# THE BEST OF ASTOUNDING

# The Best of Astounding

Edited by Tony Lewis

Baronet Publishing Company, New York

**THE BEST OF ASTOUNDING**

A Baronet Book

Second Baronet edition, June 1978



ISBN: 0-89437-024-3

Baronet Publishing Company
509 Madison Avenue
New York, N.Y. 10022

# CONTENTS

# Introduction

**By Anthony R. Lewis**

During the 1940's a series of factors converged to create a Golden Age in science fiction storytelling. Among these factors were a new group of knowledgeable writers who shared a faith that technology could solve social problems, a strong market for magazine fiction generally, and an editor who demanded competency and literacy from his writers.

That editor was John W. Campbell Jr. and his magazine was *Astounding Science Fiction,* which has since metamorphosed into *Analog* magazine.

## INTRODUCTION

This anthology, part of the Analog Books series, is a selection of stories from *Astounding*'s—and science fiction's—Golden Age.

Science fiction historians like to trace the field's roots back into the past, much as the Tudor genealogists created imaginary pedigrees for their patrons. To be honest about it, science fiction is a child of the future and the future wasn't fully invented until Victorian times. H.G. Wells, if he didn't create it, at least got a freehold lease on the future and has been pleased to let us wander about in it without calling the police. But the vandalism...

In Wells' time, science fiction, as a genre, didn't exist. In fact, genre literature didn't come into being until much later. SF stories were stories and were lumped in with everything else. This attitude is still not uncommon in England today.

Crossing the Atlantic to the New World with a young Luxembourgois named Hugo Gernsback we can begin to see SF split from the "main stream." Gernsback had a love affair with the future and the U.S. was closer to it at the turn of the century than the Continent was. Gernsback's home experimenter magazines carried science fiction, though not yet under that name. Finally, having gone through the War to End Wars, and recovered its breath, the world was ready. In 1926, the first all-SF magazine, *Amazing Stories,* was published. In those days SF was STF for scientifiction—that changed. All the genre literature eutrophied during that decade from 1926 to 1935. Genre magazines in such fields as Zeppelin Nurses came and went. By the middle 1930's there were a number of SF magazines in the field, none really worthy of note, most printing "wordwooze," entertaining reading for an evening in the depression. Something to take one's mind away from the surrounding grey mundanity.

....And then came John W. Campbell, Jr. to ASTOUNDING.

Campbell turned what was pulp into something that could become literature (whatever that may be). He demanded of his writers, internal consistency, believeability, and, above all, a story. A story about people doing something—not passively accepting what the universe threw at them. Campbell's people, and they are all his people in some way because of that, believed that problems could be solved, that intelligence and logic and goodwill and determination and hard work was the way. They were crude and mostly unaware of sensibilities and finer things. But, the bedrock has to be blasted out before any edifice can be erected.

The 1940's were a golden age of SF with such writers as Asimov, Heinlein, de Camp, del Rey, Sturgeon, Clement, Leiber, Kuttner, and Simak appearing or greatly improving. (Murray Leinster had always been there and had always written competent well-crafted stories—Jack Williamson was there before the Golden Age, is still here and writing well).

*Astounding* was the leader in the 1940's. Nothing else was even remotely in second place. 120 issues from January 1940 to December 1949—no hiatus in publication, even during the war years. During that time, aside from the efforts of such pioneers as Donald Wollheim and Groff Conklin, there were no SF anthologies. Publishers knew that SF books wouldn't sell.

When the anthologies began to appear in the 1950's and 1960's and 1970's, there was very rich ore to be mined. Of course, the "best" stories were printed, and reprinted and reprinted. The early anthologies went out of print, more followed. But now more magazines existed and more issues of *Astounding* had been published. The lesser known stories of the 40's remained in the dark. New stories filled the anthologies, anthologies even became magazine-like, publishing original stories following the too-early experiment of Frederik Pohl with *Star Science Fiction* in the 1950's. The original anthologies bloomed to excess and faded back to a reasonable rate. Magazines have been cut back to a small number still publishing good science fiction.

Why then look back to the 1940's? First, many of the acknowledged excellent works have long been out of print. It is time to bring them to the notice of a new generation of readers who either do not know of the early magazines or cannot obtain them. Second, in the thirty years that have passed we have changed. We are not as we were then and so our perception of these stories has changed. Works that might have seemed trivial or even unbelievable then take on new meaning today. Heinlein's "Solution Unsatisfactory" was much more meaningful than Cleve Cartmill's much anecdoted story describing the atomic bomb in detail. But, Heinlein's story could not really be appreciated until we had lived through the Balance of Terror of the late 1950's and early 1960's.

Finally, these stories are fun to read; some may be crude, the machinery may poke through here and there—but they are stories. They are stories which I enjoyed reading; that was the first criterion. I have tried to balance the book between light and heavy reading, between short and long works, between straight-forward and convoluted plots.

Some of you will be rereading old favorites not seen

for a long time; they have survived even as you and I and will give you enjoyment. Newer readers may be seeing these for the first time; this is a unique and enviable pleasure—savor it.

The Phoenix had one way to immortality—a painful way. No man, as an individual, is immortal, yet we are immortal through descendants. But races? They're strictly mortal—

# Letter To a Phoenix

**By Fredric Brown**
Illustrated by Orban

There is much to tell you, so much that it is difficult to know where to begin. Fortunately, I have forgotten most of the things that have happened to me. Fortunately, the mind has a limited capacity for remembering. It would be horrible if I remembered the details of a hundred and eighty thousand years—the details of four thousand lifetimes that I have lived since the first great atomic war.

Not that I have forgotten the really great moments. I remember being on the first expedition to land on Mars and the third to land on Venus. I remember—I believe it was in the third great war—the blasting of Skoro from the sky by a force that compares to nuclear fission as a nova compares to our slowly dying sun. I was second in command of a Hyper-A Class spacer in the war against the second extragalactic invaders, the ones who established bases on Jupe's moons before we knew we were there and then almost drove us out of the Solar System before we found the one weapon they couldn't stand up against. So they fled where we couldn't follow them, then, outside of the Galaxy. When we did follow them, about fifteen thousand years later, they were gone. They were dead three thousand years.

And that is what I want to tell you about—that mighty race and the others—but first, so that you will know how I know what I know, I will tell you about myself.

I am not immortal. There is only one immortal being in the universe; of it, more anon. Compared to it, I am of no importance, but you will not understand or believe what I say to you unless you understand what I am.

There is little in a name, and that is a fortunate thing—for I do not remember mine. That is less strange than you think, for a hundred and eighty thousand years is a long time and for one reason or another I have changed my name a thousand times or more. And what could matter less than the name my parents gave me a hundred and eighty thousand years ago?

I am not a mutant. What happened to me happened when I was twenty-three years old, during the first atomic war. The first war, that is, in which both sides used atomic weapons—puny weapons, of course, compared to subsequent ones. It was less than a score of years after the discovery of the atom bomb. The first bombs were dropped in a minor war while I was still a child. They ended that war quickly for only one side had them.

# LETTER TO A PHOENIX

The first atomic war wasn't a bad one—the first one never is. I was lucky for, if it had been a bad one—one which ended a civilization—I'd not have survived it despite the biological accident that happened to me. If it had ended a civilization, I wouldn't have been kept alive during the sixteen-year sleep period I went through about thirty years later. But again I get ahead of the story.

## LETTER TO A PHOENIX

I was, I believe, twenty or twenty-one years old when the war started. They didn't take me for the army right away because I was not physically fit. I was suffering from a rather rare disease of the pituitary gland—Somebody's syndrome. I've forgotten the name. It caused obesity, among other things. I was about fifty pounds overweight for my height and had little stamina. I was rejected without a second thought.

About two years later my disease had progressed slightly, but other things had progressed more than slightly. By that time the army was taking anyone; they'd have taken a one-legged one-armed blind man if he was willing to fight. And I was willing to fight. I'd lost my family in a dusting, I hated my job in a war plant, and I had been told by doctors that my disease was incurable and I had only a year or two to live in any case. So I went to what was left of the army, and what was left of the army took me without a second thought and sent me to the nearest front, which was ten miles away. I was in the fighting one day after I joined.

Now I remember enough to know that *I* hadn't anything to do with it, but it happened that the time I joined was the turn of the tide. The other side was out of bombs and dust and getting low on shells and bullets. We were out of bombs and dust, too, but they hadn't knocked out *all* of our production facilities and we'd got just about all of theirs. We still had planes to carry them, too, and we still had the semblance of an organization to send the planes to the right places. Nearly the right places, anyway; sometimes we dropped them too close to our own troops by mistake. It was a week after I'd got into the fighting that I got out of it again—knocked out of it by one of our smaller bombs that had been dropped about a mile away.

I came to, about two weeks later, in a base hospital,

The proposition in this one, gentlemen, is a dilly. And you are invited to answer the implied question, "Well—what would you do about it?"

# Cold War

**By Kris Neville**
Illustrated by Brush

The Government needs YOU! *if* you can qualify. YES! Space Stations need men! America's defense has an opening for you! *Excellent* pay!! *Generous* Furloughs! Applicants must be between the ages of 24 and 32, and must pass a rigid physical examination. For full particulars and application blanks visit or write any government post office.

"The President is in conference," the third assistant informed Leland Kreiger.

Leland Kreiger took out his calling card. It contained

nothing more than his name and the initials, XSSC, in pica type, in the lower left-hand corner. "Will you hand him this, please," he said. "He is expecting me."

"I'm sorry, Mr. . . . uh . . . Kreiger, but I must know the nature of your business."

"On the contrary; you must *not,"* Leland Kreiger said, "I assure you the President will be interested."

And ten minutes later, Leland Kreiger was seated before the President's desk.

The President was a tired man. His face showed it, his body showed it, his eyes showed it. His cheeks were hollow, his shoulders bent, and, under his eyes, there were large, black rings. He had been in office only two years.

"Mr. President. Failure."

It was a bleak statement. But the expression on his face never changed. The President took it calmly.

The President sighed. "I should have known. It was the last chance—" His voice trailed off. "You did the best you could. I don't blame you."

"I tried," Leland Kreiger said. There was nothing else to say.

"Did they believe you? Your credentials—?"

"Of course. They were certain I was your direct representative. No doubt about that."

"And they said?"

"That there are things more precious than life; that their people could never tolerate a foreign rule—" He hesitated for a moment, and then added, hastily, "And that we were bluffing."

"I expected it, of course. But I could hope. Now. . . Leland, is there no answer?"

The President asked the last much in the spirit of a man appealing to a doctor who has told him he has but three weeks to live.

"There is only one answer, sir. I was sent to tell them to submit all their armaments to us or we would destroy them. They said it was a bluff. The only thing to do is—to destroy them."

"Leland, you know I could never do that," said the President, looking down at his hands. "Perhaps the rulers, yes. But think of the innocent men, women, and children... the uncounted millions—"

He looked up. "It's strange, isn't it? If a state of war existed between us, then perhaps I would. But no such state exists. Ostensibly we are friendly nations. I might rouse our people to a point where they would support a war—but I could never justify it. The enemy will go just so far, and no further. They are careful not to give us an excuse."

He paused a moment. "How cruel it would sound: 'He could find no solution but slaughter!' If we used the weapon once, what would the world think? How could we ever *hope* for peace?"

"But sir, the risk—"

"With one hundred million lives at stake, no risk is too great! What would history say? What would all Christian instinct tell us?"

"If we only had time."

"Time? How I hate that word. Yes, yes, yes. If we only had time— In twenty or thirty years we could discontinue the Space Stations. But not now."

The President looked up at the ceiling. And beyond it. He shuddered.

## COLD WAR

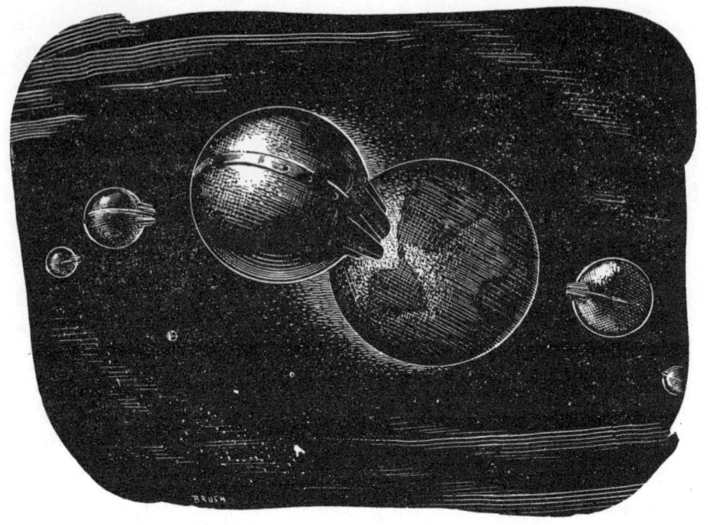


The President called in Senator Tyler of New York, leader of the opposition in Congress. The President did not like him personally. And, yet, this was not a question of personalities.

"Senator, please be seated," he said, after shaking the man's hand as warmly as possible.

The senator sat down, and, without asking, extracted a cigar. He lit it.

The President set his lips grimly. "I have asked you here on a matter of vital interest to this country. *Vital*. Anything that I tell you today is in the strictest confidence."

The senator leaned back. He did not commit himself.

The President ruffled some papers on his desk.

"I want to stress the importance of secrecy. The newspapers must never discover what I am about to tell you. It would... well, it would throw the world into a panic."

"That is very strong language, Mr. President."

The President looked him over carefully. He was a huge man. Fat. Heavy jowls. Tiny eyes. Eyes that glittered with shrewdness.

And the President wished it weren't necessary to tell him.

Outside, unknown to the senator, a secret service man was waiting for him to leave the office. From this day, the senator would be watched every hour of the day and night. His private mail would be opened—his telephones tapped—everything he said and did monitored by the secret service.

And if he started to reveal the secret, his life would be extinguished like a cupped candle.

The President stood up. "No, keep your seat," he said. "I assure you that it is not a strong statement."

He walked across the room. "Let me ask you once again to call off this investigation. If you were to say the word—"

"Mr. President, that is impossible. The people have a *right* to know," he sucked on his cigar, "that every safeguard is being taken to insure that the Space Stations are manned by loyal American citizens."

*If that were only the problem,* the President thought.

"Why," the senator went on, think of what would happen if an enemy spy managed to get control of a Station—he could wipe out half of the United States merely by flicking his wrist." Here the senator flicked ashes onto the carpet by way of emphasis.

Almost automatically the President thought, *Mrs. Thorne, the housekeeper, will be very angry.* He caught himself. Of late his mind had a tendency to rove, and to concern itself with the inconsequential.

The President said: "Let me assure you that every precaution is being taken. Each man is checked so thoroughly that we know him better than he knows himself. *Will you call off the investigation?"*

"NO! You're hiding something, and we are going to find out what! Don't forget that we have the right—"

"You win," the President said wearily. "I was afraid of it. It's not the loyalty check that you want to look into—you're after something else. Something's wrong, and you don't know quite what, but you intend to find out."

"Exactly," the senator said, smiling.

"If you go through with this investigation, it would result in publicity that we could not stand. There is a chance, because you gentlemen are so thorough, that you would discover what I am concealing. To prevent that, I am going to be frank with you. For, after all, one man is easier to bind to secrecy than fifteen. After you hear me out, I am sure that you will call off the investigation."

"I must reserve judgment," the senator told him.

"Very well. But, sir, remember that you have forced me. The responsibility, and the consequences, are yours, and yours alone."

"Naturally," the senator said. "I can look after myself."

The President walked to the wall chart. He unrolled it, and it rustled dryly.

"I am going to cover material with which you are completely familiar. You will forgive me, but it is necessary to stress a few points. But first, are you *sure*—?"

"Get on with it; I'm listening."

"These," the President said, pointing to circles in red on the map, "are our nine Space Stations. You will note that they are located so that, at every second, some station is in direct target line with every point on Earth. Due to physical considerations, the stations move very rapidly in their orbits. But this has been made to serve a military purpose. To destroy this defense network, it is necessary to destroy every station, because every station, in its orbit, comes within range of every point on Earth. One might be eliminated, or maybe even two, with our present technical knowledge, but not all nine. And each one, in the space of ninety seconds from a given signal, can blanket an area half the size of Asia with atomic destruction. Each space station *carries enough pure death to annihilate any nation on Earth!*"

He paused.

"It is a perfect defense against an atom bomb. But, at the same time, it is a negative defense. It cannot prevent this nation from being attacked. But an attacker would, at most, launch only a few dozen rockets before he was completely and utterly destroyed.

"And it is our only defense against aggression. It is all that we have. All of our atomic power is concentrated in those nine stations. If they were to be grounded tomorrow, we would be practically defenseless. Any one of several countries could conquer us within the space of weeks."

The President let the chart snap back on its roller.

"In effect, we rule the world. But, as you know, our 'rule' is of a negative sort. We rule by threat." He laughed dryly. "We have something hanging over their heads. They—the enemy, shall I say?—knows that we will never take positive action without strong justification—without what must amount to an open declaration of war upon us, or a definitely aggressive move against one of her weak neighbors. Therefore, the enemy has a wide range of free action.

Their only consideration is this: 'Will America use the Space Stations to stop us?', and if the answer is 'no', then they may proceed."

He looked down at the senator.

"The international situation has become pretty much of a touch and go affair. Bluff and counter bluff."

"I know all that," the senator replied.

"You will recall, also, the only time that we used a Space Station. The whole world shuddered."

"Of course. Who doesn't remember? Russia was bent on setting up a Space Station of her own. We warned her. But she thought it was a bluff. The day they were ready to launch it, we dropped a single bomb on it. After all, we couldn't permit another nation to have a Station. It would be intolerable."

"Yes," the President said, musingly, "one tiny bomb. Not an attack—but only one bomb. And yet the feeling ran high against us. Both here and abroad. The people of the world felt that surely some other means could have been found. Not involving death!"

The President sighed. "It postponed for ten years at least the day when we would no longer need Space Stations."

The President walked over and sat down.

"Russia, you will remember, protested to the U.N. She wanted the Stations placed under international control. We could not permit that, because, primarily, the Stations are not a method of enforcing peace, but of defending our own country against any and all aggressors. Russia could take no further action—for she existed only under our sufferance. She had merely gambled and lost."

"I, and any high school child," the senator said, "know that. Please come to the point."

The President ignored him. "The whole problem of Space Stations is too much for one man. I wish that I had never heard of them!"

The senator put out his cigar.

"Well, senator, let me review.

"You realize that Space Stations are our only defense?"

The senator grunted. "Yes."

"And that we cannot use them offensively against an enemy unless she gives us ample justification?"

"Yes."

"And do you know that if we discontinued them, we would be attacked tomorrow? By a nation who would absorb a calculated amount of destruction in order to dominate the world—by a ruthless enemy, an enemy who bears us not the slightest love?"

The senator snorted.

And the President smiled. "Of course," he said, "we could surrender to the enemy."

The senator jerked upright. It was an effort that made his face red. "Man, do you realize what you're saying?"

"Calm down," the President advised. "I know my oath of office as well as you do."

He hesitated a moment while the senator settled back somewhat uneasily.

"What I have done is merely mention various alternatives that would confront us if we decided to discontinue the Space Stations. Bloodshed or subjugation. The alternatives are all untenable."

"Naturally," the senator said.

"But I must discontinue the Space Stations," the President told him as mildly as if he were mentioning that eggs were on the White House breakfast menu for tomorrow.

"That will be impossible for many years," the senator said with equal mildness.

"Oh, but I don't have many years, senator. In fact I don't have any time at all."

The President got up again and walked over to the far wall and stood looking at a picture of President Lincoln. He put his hands behind his back and seemed to be talking, not to the senator, but to the picture, "Now you can begin to appreciate my position."

Adam Kregg had, for a long time, been covering the national picture, as it looked from Washington, in his daily column. Recently he had been writing on the seriousness of the military situation, and of repeated rumors "from high official sources" that the United States was planning to attack the enemy without warning. He deplored these reports, as a matter of course. He pointed out that, at present, we were in no danger; indeed, that we were able to keep peace, although an uneasy sort of peace, and that since affairs couldn't get worse, they were bound to get better. "It is possible," he wrote, "that within the next twenty years, if we continue on our present policy, differences between both nations may be resolved. At any rate, it is obvious that we can gain nothing by the use of force; it can only result in needless bloodshed. It is not justifiable. Eventually every nation will see, by our judicious use of the Space Stations, that we do not seek to rule, but that we do seek to live in Peace, unmolested by *any* aggressor."

Undoubtedly, Mr. Kregg had the welfare of man at

heart. However, he was, first and foremost, a reporter. He had an unfailing nose for news. He could put 2 and 2 and 2 and 2 together every time and come up with the correct total. A hint here, a word there, an omission elsewhere, and Adam Kregg had a scoop.

Washington was honeycombed with his sources. And nothing was sacred. If it was startling, if it would set well in type, then Mr. Kregg put it in his column.

Several times he had roused the wrath of the government. They called him irresponsible. Others called him a brave and fearless reporter. And his motto was: "All the News." Period. He would rather chop off his two hands than suppress a story.

To him nothing was confidential. Everything was grist for his mill.

Once the government sought to bring a criminal action against him. The nation's press took up the hew and cry: "If convicted, this will mean the end of a free press in America."

And Adam Kregg went happily on his way, reporting "all the news." That is, until he happened across the most closely guarded of government secrets.

Perhaps he deduced it. Perhaps someone told him. At any rate, he found out.

It was shocking. It even stunned him. He became frightened. And then he saw the story in headlines—the nation and the world thrown into the same state of terror that he was in. Naturally he decided to print it.

He was going to give it to the great American public. But if not in print, then by some other means. That was that. Arrest him, and it would come out at his trial. Any action the government chose to take, *still* the people were going to be told.

For, as Adam Kregg knew, he lived in a democracy. And the government tactics did not include—

He tucked the column into his coat pocket. He was going to take it to the syndicate personally. He was going to see it go out over the wires. And nobody was going to talk him out of it. It was the scoop of a lifetime. Maybe ten lifetimes. Better, even, than when the reporter had discovered, during the last war, that the Government had broken the Japanese code.

He got into his car and drove crosstown to the syndicate branch office.

He got out and started across the sidewalk.

A huge, black car hurtled around the corner and flashed by him. Two shotgun blasts erupted from it.

He fell, his chest torn away. He squirmed once and died.

Almost immediately, a plainclothes agent was bending over him. The man removed the bloody sheaf of typed paper. He stood up and flashed his badge to the crowd.

"This man is dead," he said.

And a policeman came running up.

The FBI seized all of Adam Kregg's personal papers. They told the press that they were looking for clues.

And there were headlines:

FBI STARTS INVESTIGATION
OF ADAM KREGG'S DEATH!

But the assassin was never found.

Adam Kregg failed to realize that the secret was too big to protect by normal, democratic procedures.

• • •

"It's a neat legal question," the Chief Psychiatrist admitted. "But you know very well we can never bring the case to court!"

The President agreed. "You're right, of course." He looked off into space. "And I hate it! The way it forces us to abridge all human rights—"

The Chief Psychiatrist nodded grimly.

"Well?" the President demanded. "Can't you *do* something? Isn't there any test? Anything?"

"No." The Chief Psychiatrist looked away. "There is no way of telling who's susceptible and who isn't. Frankly, we're puzzled. The first case came up a little over a year ago. This is the fifth. Each case follows the same pattern ... I... well, that's all we know."

"How is the man now?"

"Aside from the memory blank, completely normal."

"And what do you recommend?"

"We can't take the case to court. As it stands, of course, we can't release him. If for no other reason than security. It's obvious that he can't be held accountable—but, as I said, that's a neat legal question. And, we must remember, that the condition may return at any time."

"Well?"

"Wait and see. What else *can* we do?"

There was a momentary pause. "Mr. President, I'd like to have you see for yourself what you're up against. Come and look at the patient."

The President stood up. It was the last thing in the world that he wanted to do. But after all, this whole mess was his responsibility.

• • •

## COLD WAR

The patient was isolated in a cell block of the Federal Prison. He was sitting on his bed in the far cell.

The keys grated harshly as the jailer admitted the President and the Chief Psychiatrist.

The patient stood up. His face was pallid. Tight anguish lines laced it. But it was still a handsome face—young, strong, tanned. The eyes were red rimmed, as if the man had been crying. Blond hair spread in an unruly thatch.

The President walked slowly to his cell.

The patient looked at him for a moment without recognition. Then the red circled eyes seemed to light up.

"You're . . . you're the President!" he gasped.

"I am," the President said gently.

"I . . . I," he began and then stopped with a choke. Suddenly a wild look came into his eyes. "Why have they got me here?" He grabbed the bars and shook them. "Why? Why? WHY?" He sobbed. "Why won't they let me see my wife and baby? Why won't they let me see anybody? You're the President," his voice began almost to whine, "surely *you* can tell me. What have I done?"

He banged his fists on the bars.

"Tell me! Tell me!"

"Here, here," the Chief Psychiatrist said. "Control yourself!"

"I'm . . . I'm sorry. But why won't somebody tell me anything? I . . . I want to see Doris." He turned his face to the President. "That's my wife, sir. And Jerry. That's my baby—cutest little kid. *Why won't they let me see them?"*

He began to cry.

The Chief Psychiatrist touched the President's arm. "Let's go," he whispered. "We can't do anything. It's shock."

They turned and started to leave.

"NO!" the blond youth cried. "Oh, no! Don't leave me. Don't leave me here alone." He began to sob. "I'm afraid . . . afraid . . . afraid—"

• • •

"Doesn't he remember?" the President asked when they were out of the cell block.

"Doesn't seem to. He must have established a subconscious block. There is no conscious memory for the whole period."

"How do you explain it?"

"I can't. And what makes it more horrible, it happened after that poor kid's first tour of duty. Now we know it isn't necessarily the time element. And that's about all we know.

"Our tests are as perfect as human science can make them. We may screen as many as ten thousand applicants before we have found one who is qualified, even, for the solitary test. I'll bet we've screened half of the available men in America. We have been so selective that, if we went one step further, we could qualify no one. And yet—there is the human element there, that eludes us.

"There still remains those men upon whom the Space Stations act as a drug. Like marijuana. They seem to tower above mortality!

"And all that responsibility, all that tension—so many lives at their fingertips. And the suspense—what, with the way the newspapers are playing up the international situation—sitting there, waiting, waiting, waiting. Listening for that deadly signal. Waiting to punch the controls that will destroy one hundred million people. One-hundred-million! And the tension mounting as they swirl over enemy territory . . . the flood of relief over their own—" He paused.

"I can imagine what the poor devils must think. Life and death . . . *life* and death . . . life and *death*— Over and over, producing a hypnotic effect—like the individual death-wish. And the mind falls into that pattern—starts working like a pump."

He paused for a moment. "And then there is the second stage. 'Suppose I should push this button here, what would happen? would *happen?* would h-a-p-p-e-n? Or this button . . . or this—Life *and* death. And one-hundred-million people . . . living . . . loving—'" He stopped. "You see?"

"I—see," said the President.

"No wonder they break. All the world, all that living, there, at their fingertips—" He sighed.

"All five of the men waited until they were home on furlough before they snapped." He snapped his fingers. "Like that! And all followed a pattern—like that poor boy in there, taking a butcher knife to his wife and kid. Insane—criminally insane. Or the one before—"

"Don't!" the President ordered, closing his eyes. "Please. No more."

Then after a while, he opened his eyes again and looked upward.

The law of averages, he thought, is catching up with us. Five on furlough. And swirling in one of those nine orbits, up there, is a man who may, at any moment, become . . . just like the five . . . murderous . . . insane!

And in each of the Stations there is enough power to destroy half a continent.

# COLD WAR

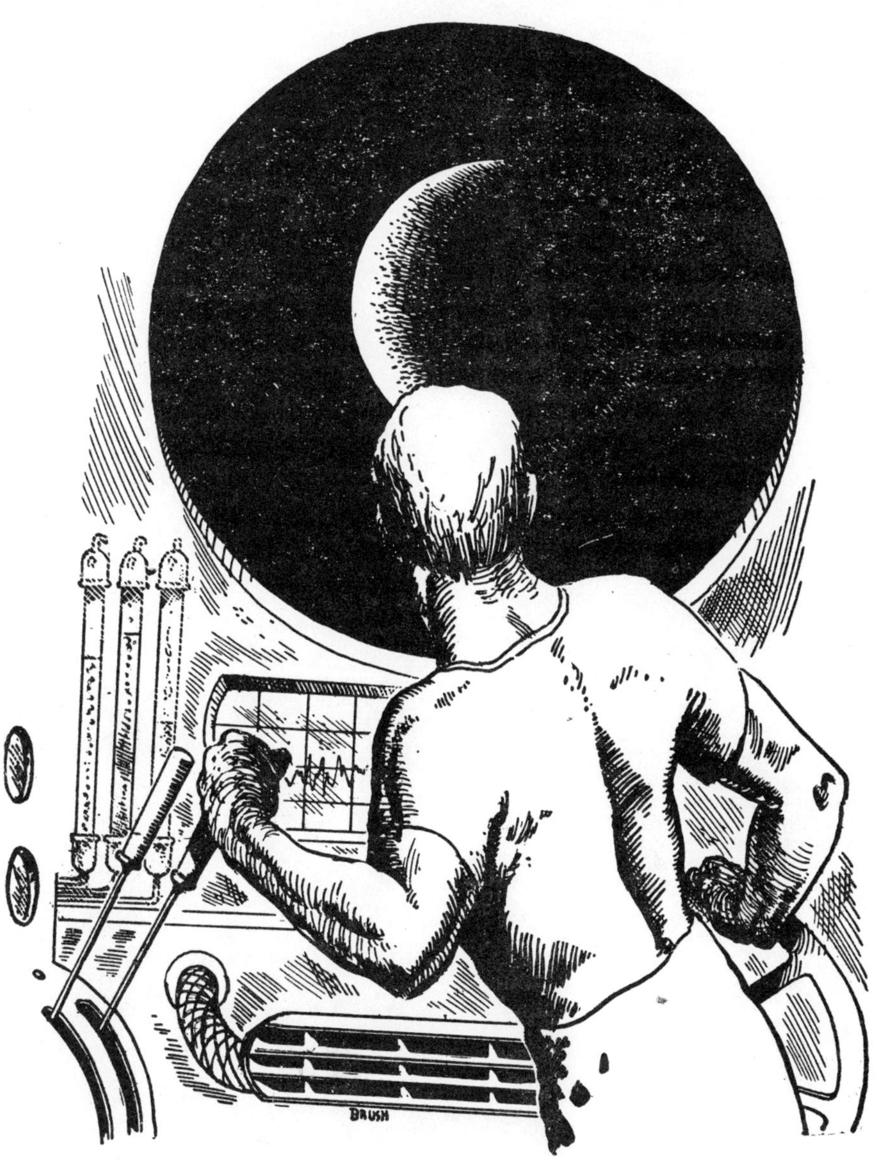

Gallegher, the Mad Scientist who plays by ear is loose! Worse—from Gallegher's viewpoint—a "small brown animal" he couldn't see kept him in a horrid state of sobriety by drinking all his liquor!

# Ex Machina

**By Lewis Padgett**
Illustrated by Cartler

"I got the idea out of a bottle labeled 'DRINK ME,'" Gallegher said wanly. "I'm no technician, except when I'm drunk. I don't know the difference between an electron and an electrode, except that one's invisible. At least I do know, sometimes, but they get mixed up. My trouble is semantics."

"Your trouble is you're a lush," said the transparent robot, crossing its legs with a faint crash. Gallegher winced.

"Not at all. I get along fine when I'm drinking. It's only during my periods of sobriety that I get confused. I have a technological hangover. The aqueous humor in my eyeballs is coming out by osmosis. Does that make sense?"

"No," said the robot, whose name was Joe. "You're crying, that's all. Did you turn me on just to have an audience? I'm busy at the moment."

"Busy with what?"

"I'm analyzing philosophy, *per se*. Hideous as you humans are, you sometimes get bright ideas. The clear, intellectual logic of pure philosophy is a revelation to me."

Gallegher said something about a hard, gemlike flame. He still wept sporadically, which reminded him of the bottle labeled "DRINK ME," which reminded him of the liquor-organ beside the couch. Gallegher stiffly moved his long body across the laboratory, detouring around three bulky objects which might have been the dynamos, Monstro and Bubbles, except for the fact that there were three of them. This realization flickered only dimly through Gallegher's mind. Since one of the dynamos was looking at him, he hurriedly averted his gaze, sank down on the couch, and manipulated several buttons. When no liquor flowed through the tube into his parched mouth, he removed the mouthpiece, blinked at it hopelessly, and ordered Joe to bring beer.

The glass was brimming as he raised it to his lips. But it was empty before he drank.

"That's very strange," Gallegher said. "I feel like Tantalus."

"Somebody's drinking your beer," Joe explained. "Now do leave me alone. I've an idea I'll be able to appreciate my baroque beauty even more after I've mastered the essentials of philosophy."

"No doubt," Gallegher said. "Come away from that mirror. Who's drinking my beer? A little green man?"

"A little brown animal," Joe explained cryptically, and

turned to the mirror again, leaving Gallegher to glare at him hatefully. There were times when Mr. Galloway Gallegher yearned to bind Joe securely under a steady drip of hydrochloric. Instead, he tried another beer, with equal ill luck.

In a sudden fury, Gallegher rose and procured soda water. The little brown animal had even less taste for such fluids than Gallegher himself; at any rate, the water didn't mysteriously vanish. Less thirsty but more confused than ever, Gallegher circled the third dynamo with the bright blue eyes and morosely examined the equipment littering his workbench. There were bottles filled with ambiguous liquids, obviously nonalcoholic, but the labels meant little or nothing. Gallegher's subconscious self, liberated by liquor

last night, had marked them for easy reference. Since Gallegher Plus, though a top-flight technician, saw the world through thoroughly distorted lenses, the labels were not helpful. One said "RABBITS ONLY." Another inquired "WHY NOT?" A third said "CHRISTMAS NIGHT."

There was also a complicated affair of wheels, gears, tubes, sprockets and light tubes plugged into an electric outlet.

*"Cogito, ergo sum,"* Joe murmured softly. "When there's no one around on the quad. No. Hm-m-m."

"What about this little brown animal?" Gallegher wanted to know. "Is it real or merely a figment?"

"What is reality?" Joe inquired, thus confusing the issue still further. "I haven't resolved that yet to my own satisfaction."

"Your satisfaction!" Gallegher said. "I wake up with a tenth-power hangover and you can't get a drink. You tell me fairy stories about little brown animals stealing my liquor. Then you quote moldy philosophical concepts at me. If I pick up that crowbar over there, you'll neither be *nor* think, in very short order."

Joe gave ground gracefully. "It's a small creature that moves remarkably fast. So fast it can't be seen."

"How come you see it?"

"I don't. I varish it," said Joe, who had more than the five senses normal to humans.

"Where is it now?"

"It went out a while ago."

"Well—" Gallegher sought inconclusively for words. "Something must have happened last night."

"Naturally," Joe agreed. "But you turned me off after the ugly man with the ears came in."

"I remember that. You were beating your plastic gums . . . *what* man?"

"The ugly one. You told your grandfather to take a walk, too, but you couldn't pry him loose from his bottle."

"Grandpa. Uh. Oh. Where's he?"

"Maybe he went back to Maine," Joe suggested. "He kept threatening to do that."

"He never leaves till he's drunk out the cellar," Gallegher said. He tuned in the audio system and called every room in the house. There was no response. Presently Gallegher got up and made a search. There was no trace of Grandpa.

He came back to the laboratory, trying to ignore the third dynamo with the big blue eyes, and hopelessly studied the workbench again. Joe, posturing before the mirror, said he thought he believed in the basic philosophy of intellectualism. Still, he added, since obviously Gallegher's intellect was in abeyance, it might pay to hook up the projector and find out what had happened last night.

This made sense. Some time before, realizing that Gallegher sober never remembered the adventures of Gallegher tight, he had installed a visio-audio gadget in the laboratory, cleverly adjusted to turn itself on whenever circumstances warranted it. How the thing worked Gallegher wasn't quite sure anymore, except that it could run off miraculous blood-alcohol tests on its creator and start recording when the percentage was sufficiently high. At the moment the machine was shrouded in a blanket. Gallegher whipped this off, wheeled over a screen, and watched and listened to what had happened last night.

Joe stood in a corner, turned off, probably cogitating.

## EX MACHINA

Grandpa, a wizened little man with a brown face like a bad-tempered nutcracker, sat on a stool cuddling a bottle. Gallegher was removing the liquor-organ mouthpiece from between his lips, having just taken on enough of a load to start the recorder working.

A slim, middle-aged man with large ears and an eager expression jittered on the edge of his relaxer, watching Gallegher.

"Claptrap," Grandpa said in a squeaky voice. "When I was a kid we went out and killed grizzlies with our hands. None of these new-fangled ideas—"

"Grandpa," Gallegher said, "shut up. You're not that old. And you're a liar anyway."

"Reminds me of the time I was out in the woods and a grizzly came at me. I didn't have a gun. Well, I'll tell you. I just reached down his mouth—"

"Your bottle's empty," Gallegher said cleverly, and there was a pause while Grandpa, startled, investigated. It wasn't.

"You were highly recommended," said the eager man. "I do hope you can help me. My partner and I are about at the end of our rope."

Gallegher looked at him dazedly. "You have a partner? Who's he? For that matter, who are you?"

Dead silence fell while the eager man fought with his bafflement. Grandpa lowered his bottle and said: "It wasn't empty, but it is now. Where's another?"

The eager man blinked. "Mr. Gallegher," he said faintly. "I don't understand. We've been discussing—"

Gallegher said, "I know. I'm sorry. It's just that I'm no good on technical problems unless I'm . . . ah . . . stimulated. Then I'm a genius. But I'm awfully absent-minded. I'm sure

I can solve your problem, but the fact is I've forgotten what it is. I suggest you start from the beginning. Who are you and have you given me any money yet?"

"I'm Jonas Harding," the eager man said. "I've got fifty thousand credits in my pocket, but we haven't come to any terms yet."

"Then give me the dough and we'll come to terms," Gallegher said with ill-concealed greed. "I need money."

"You certainly do," Grandpa put in, searching for a bottle. "You're so overdrawn at the bank that they lock the doors when they see you coming. I want a drink."

"Try the organ," Gallegher suggested. "Now, Mr. Harding—"

"I want a bottle. I don't trust that dohinkus of yours."

Harding, for all his eagerness, could not quite conceal a growing skepticism. "As for the credits," he said, "I think perhaps we'd better talk a little first. You were very highly recommended, but perhaps this is one of your off days."

"Not at all. Still—"

"Why should I give you the money before we come to terms?" Harding pointed out. "Especially since you've forgotten who I am and what I wanted."

Gallegher sighed and gave up. "All right. Tell me what you are and who you want. I mean—"

"I'll go back home," Grandpa threatened. "Where's a bottle?"

Harding said desperately, "Look, Mr. Gallegher, there's a limit. I come in here and that robot of yours insults me. Your grandfather insists I have a drink with him. I'm nearly poisoned—"

"I was weaned on corn likker," Grandpa muttered. "Young whippersnappers can't take it."

"Then let's get down to business," Gallegher said brightly. "I'm beginning to feel good. I'll just relax here on the couch and you can tell me everything." He relaxed and sucked idly at the organ's mouthpiece, which trickled a gin buck. Grandpa cursed.

"Now," Gallegher said, "the whole thing, from the beginning."

Harding gave a little sigh. "Well—I'm half partner in Adrenals, Incorporated. We run a service. A luxury service, keyed to this day and age. As I told you—"

"I've forgotten it all," Gallegher murmured. "You should have made a carbon copy. What is it you do? I've got a mad picture of you building tiny prefabricated houses on top of kidneys, but I know I must be wrong."

"You are," Harding said shortly. "Here's your carbon copy. We're in the adrenal-rousing business. Today man lives a quiet, safe life—"

"Ha!" Gallegher interjected bitterly.

"—what with safety controls and devices, medical advances, and the general structure of social living. Now the adrenal glands serve a vital functional purpose, necessary to the health of the normal man." Harding had apparently launched into a familiar sales talk. "Ages ago we lived in caves, and when a sabertooth burst out of the jungle, our adrenals, or suprarenals, went into instant action, flooding our systems with adrenalin. There was an immediate explosion of action, either toward fight or flight, and such periodic flooding of the blood stream gave tone to the whole system. Not to mention the psychological advantages. Man is a competitive animal. He's losing that instinct, but it can be roused by artificial stimulation of the adrenals."

"A drink?" Grandpa said hopefully, though he understood practically nothing of Harding's explanation.

Harding's face became shrewder. He leaned forward confidentially.

"Glamour," he said. "That's the answer. We offer adventure. Safe, thrilling, dramatic, exciting, glamorous adventure to the jaded modern man or woman. Not the vicarious, unsatisfactory excitement of television; the real article. Adrenals, Incorporated, will give you adventure plus, and at the same time improve your health physically and mentally. You must have seen our ads: 'Are you in a rut? Are you jaded? Take a Hunt—and return refreshed, happy, and healthy, ready to lick the world!'"

"A Hunt?"

"That's our most popular service," Harding said, relapsing into more businesslike tones. "It's not new, really. A long time ago travel bureaus were advertising thrilling tiger hunts in Mexico—"

"Ain't no tigers in Mexico," Grandpa said. "I been there. I warn you, if you don't find me a bottle, I'm going right back to Maine."

But Gallegher was concentrating on the problem. "I don't see why you need me, then. I can't supply tigers for you."

"The Mexican tiger was really a member of the cat family. Puma, I think. We've got special reservations all over the world—expensive to set up and maintain—and there we have our Hunts, with every detail carefully planned in advance. The danger must be minimized—in fact, eliminated. But there must be an illusion of danger or there's no thrill for the customer. We've tried conditioning animals so they'll stop short of hurting anyone, but . . . ah . . . that isn't too successful. We lost several customers, I'm sorry to say. This is an enormous investment, and we've got to recoup. But we've found we can't use tigers or, in fact, any of the large carnivora. It simply isn't safe. But there must be that illusion of danger! The trouble is, we're degenerating into a trapshooting club. And there's no personal danger involved in trapshooting."

Grandpa said: "Want some fun, eh? Come on up to Maine with me and I'll show you some real hunting. We still got bear back in the mountains."

Gallegher said: "I'm beginning to see. But that personal angle—I wonder! What is the definition of danger, anyhow?"

"Danger's when something's trying to git you," Grandpa pointed out.

"The unknown—the strange—is dangerous too, simply because we don't understand it. That's why ghost stories have always been popular. A roar in the dark is more frightening than a tiger in the daylight."

Harding nodded. "I see your point. But there's another factor. The game mustn't be made too easy. It's a cinch to outwit a rabbit. And, naturally, we have to supply our customers with the most modern weapons."

"Why?"

"Safety precautions. The trouble is, with those weapons and scanners and scent-analyzers, any fool can track down and kill an animal. There's no thrill involved unless the animal's a man-eating tiger, and that's a little too thrilling for our underwriters!"

"So what do you want?"

"I'm not sure," Harding said slowly. "A new animal, perhaps. One that fulfills the requirements of Adrenals, Incorporated. But I'm not sure what the answer is, or I wouldn't be asking you."

Gallegher said: "You don't make new animals out of thin air."

"Where do you get them?"

"I wonder. Other planets? Other time-sectors? Other probability-worlds? I got hold of some funny animals once—Lybblas—by tuning in on a future time-era on Mars, but they wouldn't have filled the bill."

"Other planets, then?"

Gallegher got up and strolled to his workbench. He began to piece together stray cogs and tubes. "I'm getting a thought. The latent factors inherent in the human brain— My latent factors are rousing to life. Let me see. Perhaps—"

Under his hands a gadget grew. Gallagher remained preoccupied. Presently he cursed, tossed the device aside, and settled back to the liquor-organ. Grandpa had already tried it, but choked on his first sip of a gin buck. He threatened to go back home and take Harding with him and show him some real hunting.

Gallegher pushed the old gentleman off the couch. "Now look, Mr. Harding," he said. "I'll have this for you tomorrow. I've got some thinking to do—"

"Drinking, you mean," Harding said, taking out a bundle of credits. "I've heard a lot about you, Mr. Gallegher. You never work except under pressure. You've got to have a deadline, or you won't do a thing. Well—do you see this? Fifty thousand credits." He glanced at his wrist watch. "I'm giving you one hour. If you don't solve my problem by then, the deal's off."

Gallegher started up from the couch as though he had been bitten. "That's ridiculous. An hour isn't time enough—"

Harding said obdurately: "I'm a methodical man. I know enough about you to realize that you're not. I can find other specialists and technicians, you know. One hour! Or I go out that door and take these fifty thousand credits with me!"

Gallegher eyed the money greedily. He took a quick drink, cursed quietly, and went back to his gadget. This time he kept working on it.

After a while a light shot up from the worktable and hit Gallegher in the eye. He staggered back, yelping.

"Are you all right?" Harding asked, jumping up.

"Sure," Gallegher growled, cutting a switch. "I think I'm getting it. That light...ouch. I've sunburned my eyeballs." He blinked back tears. Then he went over to the liquor-organ.

After a hearty swig, he nodded at Harding. "I'm getting on the trail of what you want. I don't know how long it will take, though." He winced. "Grandpa. Did you change the setting on this thing?"

"I dunno. I pushed some buttons."

"I thought so. This isn't a gin buck. Wheeooo!"

"Got a wallop, has it?" Grandpa said, getting interested and coming over to try the liquor-organ again.

"Not at all," Gallegher said, walking on his knees toward the audio-sonic recorder. "What's this? A spy, huh? We know how to deal with spies in this house, you dirty traitor." So saying, he rose to his feet, seized a blanket, and threw it over the projector.

At that point the screen, naturally enough, was blank.

• • •

"I cleverly outwit myself every time," Gallegher remarked, rising to switch off the projector. "I go to the trouble of building that recorder and then blindfold it just when matters get interesting. I know less than I did before, because there are more unknown factors now."

"Men can know the nature of things," Joe murmured.

"An important concept," Gallegher admitted. "The Greeks found it out quite a while ago, though. Pretty soon, if you keep on thinking hard, you'll come up with the bright discovery that two and two are four."

"Be quiet, you ugly man," Joe said. "I'm getting into abstractions now. Answer the door and leave me alone."

"The door? Why? The bell isn't singing."

"It will," Joe pointed out. "There it goes."

"Visitors at this time of the morning," Gallegher sighed. "Maybe it's Grandpa, though." He pushed a button, studied the doorplate screen, and failed to recognize the lantern-jawed, bushy-browed face. "All right," he said. "Come in. Follow the guide-line." Then he turned to the liquor-organ thirstily before remembering his current Tantalus proclivities.

The lantern-jawed man came into the room. Gallegher said: "Hurry up. I'm being followed by a little brown animal that drinks all my liquor. I've several other troubles, too, but the little brown animal's the worst. If I don't get a drink, I'll die. So tell me what you want and leave me alone to work out my problems. I don't owe you money, do I?"

"That depends," said the newcomer, with a strong Scots accent. "My name is Murdoch Mackenzie, and I assume you're Mr. Gallegher. You look untrustworthy. Where is my partner and the fifty thousand credits he had with him?"

Gallegher pondered. "Your partner, eh? I wonder if you mean Jonas Harding?"

"That's the lad. My partner in Adrenals, Incorporated."

"I haven't seen him—"

With his usual felicity, Joe remarked, "The ugly man with the big ears. How hideous he was."

"Vurra true," Mackenzie nodded. "I note you're using the past tense, or rather that great clanking machine of yours is. Have you perhaps murdered my partner and disposed of his body with one of your scientific gadgets?"

"Now look—" Gallegher said. "What's the idea? Have I got the mark of Cain on my forehead or something? Why should you jump to a conclusion like that? You're crazy."

Mackenzie rubbed his long jaw and studied Gallegher from under his bushy gray brows. "It would be no great loss, I know," he admitted. "Jonas is little help in the business. Too methodical. But he had fifty thousand credits on his person when he came here last night. There is also the question of the body. The insurance is perfectly enormous. Between ourselves, Mr. Gallegher, I would not hold it against you if you had murdered my unfortunate partner and pocketed the fifty thousand. In fact, I would be willing to consider letting you escape with . . . say . . . ten thousand, provided you gave me the rest. But not unless you provided me with legal evidence of Jonas's death, so my underwriters would be satisfied."

"Logic," Joe said admiringly. "Beautiful logic. It's amazing that such logic should come from such an opaque horror."

"I would look far more horrible, my friend, if I had a transparent skin like you," Mackenzie said, "if the anatomy charts are accurate. But we were discussing the matter of my partner's body."

Gallegher said wildly: "This is fantastic. You're probably laying yourself open to compounding a felony or something."

"Then you admit the charge."

"Of course not! You're entirely too sure of yourself, Mr. Mackenzie. I'll bet you killed Harding yourself and you're trying to frame me for it. How do you know he's dead?"

"Now that calls for some explanation, I admit," Mackenzie said. "Jonas was a methodical man. Vurra. I have never known him to miss an appointment for any reason whatsoever. He had appointments last night, and more this morning. One with me. Moreover, he had fifty thousand credits on him when he came here to see you last night."

"How do you know he got here?"

"I brought him, in my aircab. I let him out at your door. I saw him go in."

"Well, you didn't see him go out, but he did," Gallegher said.

Mackenzie, quite unruffled, went on checking points on his bony fingers.

"This morning I checked your record, Mr. Gallegher, and it is not a good one. Unstable, to say the least. You have been mixed up in some shady deals, and you have been accused of crimes in the past. Nothing was ever proved, but you're a sly one, I suspect. The police would agree."

"They can't prove a thing. Harding's probably home in bed."

"He is not. Fifty thousand credits is a lot of money. My partner's insurance amounts to much more than that. The business will be tied up sadly if Jonas remains vanished, and there will be litigation. Litigation costs money."

"I didn't kill your partner!" Gallegher cried.

"Ah," Mackenzie smiled. "Still, if I can prove that you did, it will come to the same thing, and be reasonably profitable for me. You see your position, Mr. Gallegher. Why not admit it, tell me what you did with the body, and escape with five thousand credits."

"You said ten thousand a while ago."

"You're daft," Mackenzie said firmly. "I said nothing of the sort. At least, you canna prove that I did."

Gallegher said: "Well, suppose we have a drink and talk it over." A new idea had struck him.

"An excellent suggestion."

Gallegher found two glasses and manipulated the liquor-organ. He offered one drink to Mackenzie, but the man shook his head and reached for the other glass. "Poison, perhaps," he said cryptically. "You have an untrustworthy face."

Gallegher ignored that. He was hoping that with two drinks available, the mysterious little brown animal would show its limitations. He tried to gulp the whisky fast, but only a tantalizing drop burned on his tongue. The glass was empty. He lowered it and stared at Mackenzie.

"A cheap trick," Mackenzie said, putting his own glass down on the workbench. "I did not ask for your whisky, you know. How did you make it disappear like that?"

Furious with disappointment, Gallegher snarled: "I'm a wizard. I've sold my soul to the devil. For two cents I'd make you disappear, too."

Mackenzie shrugged. "I am not worried. If you could,

# EX MACHINA

you'd have done it before this. As for wizardry, I am far from skeptical, after seeing that monster squatting over there." He indicated the third dynamo that wasn't a dynamo.

"What? You mean you see it, too?"

"I see more than you think, Mr. Gallegher," Mackenzie said darkly. "In fact, I am going to the police now."

"Wait a minute. You can't gain anything by that—"

"I can gain nothing by talking to you. Since you remain obdurate, I will try the police. If they can prove that Jonas is dead, I will at least collect his insurance."

Gallegher said: "Now wait a minute. Your partner did come here. He wanted me to solve a problem for him."

"Ah. And you solved it?"

"N-no. At least—"

"Then I can get no profit from you," Mackenzie said firmly, and turned to the door. "You will hear from me vurra soon."

He departed. Gallegher sank down miserably on the couch and brooded. Presently he lifted his eyes to stare at the third dynamo.

It was not, then, a hallucination, as he had first suspected. Nor was it a dynamo. It was a squat, shapeless object like a truncated pyramid that had begun to melt down, and two large blue eyes were watching him. Eyes, or agates, or painted metal. He couldn't be sure. It was about three feet high and three feet in diameter at the base.

"Joe," Gallegher said, "why didn't you tell me about that thing?"

"I thought you saw it," Joe explained.

"I did, but—what is it?"

"I haven't the slightest idea."

"Where could it have come from?"

"Your subconscious alone knows what you were up to last night," Joe said. "Perhaps Grandpa and Jonas Harding know, but they're not around, apparently."

Gallegher went to the teleview and put in a call to Maine. "Grandpa may have gone back home. It isn't likely he'd have taken Harding with him, but we can't miss any bets. I'll check on that. One thing, my eyes have stopped watering. What *was* that gadget I made last night?" He passed to the workbench and studied the cryptic assemblage. "I wonder why I put a shoehorn in that circuit?"

"If you'd keep a supply of materials available here, Gallegher Plus wouldn't have to depend on makeshifts," Joe said severely.

"Uh. I could get drunk and let my subconscious take over again...no, I can't. Joe, I can't drink anymore! I'm bound hand and foot to the water wagon!"

"I wonder if Dalton had the right idea after all?"

Gallegher snarled: "Do you have to extrude your eyes that way? I need help!"

"You won't get it from me," Joe said. "The problem's extremely simple, if you'd put your mind to it."

"Simple, is it? Then suppose you tell me the answer!"

"I want to be sure of a certain philosophical concept first."

"Take all the time you want. When I'm rotting in jail, you can spend your leisure hours pondering abstracts. *Get me a beer!* No, never mind. I couldn't drink it anyway. What does this little brown animal look like?"

"Oh, use your head," Joe said.

Gallegher growled, “I could use it for an anchor, the way it feels. You know all the answers. Why not tell me instead of babbling?”

“Men can know the nature of things,” Joe said. “Today is the logical development of yesterday. Obviously you’ve solved the problem Adrenals, Incorporated, gave you.”

“What? Oh. I see. Harding wanted a new animal or something.”

“Well?”

“I’ve got two of ’em,” Gallegher said. “That little brown invisible dipsomaniac and that blue-eyed critter sitting on the floor. Oh-*ho!* Where did I pick them up? Another dimension?”

“How should I know? You’ve got ’em.”

“I’ll say I have,” Gallegher agreed. “Maybe I made a machine that scooped them off another world—and maybe Grandpa and Harding are on that world now! A sort of exchange of prisoners. I don’t know. Harding wanted non-dangerous beasts elusive enough to give hunters a thrill—but where’s the element of danger?” He gulped. “Conceivably the pure alienage of the critters provides that illusion. Anyway, I’m shivering.”

“Flooding of the blood stream with adrenalin gives tone to the whole system,” Joe said smugly.

“So I captured or got hold of those beasts somehow, apparently, to solve Harding’s problem . . . mm-m.” Gallegher went to stand in front of the shapeless blue-eyed creature. “Hey, you,” he said.

There was no response. The mild blue eyes continued to regard nothing. Gallegher poked a finger tentatively at one of them.

Nothing at all happened. The eye was immovable and

hard as glass. Gallegher tried the thing's bluish, sleek skin. It felt like metal. Repressing his mild panic, he tried to lift the beast from the floor, but failed completely. It was either enormously heavy or it had sucking-disks on its bottom.

"Eyes," Gallegher said. "No other sensory organs, apparently. That isn't what Harding wanted."

"I think it clever of the turtle," Joe suggested.

"Turtle? Oh. Like the armadillo. That's right. It's a problem, isn't it? How can you kill or capture a . . . a beast like this? Its exoderm feels plenty hard, it's immovable—that's it, Joe. Quarry doesn't have to depend on flight or fight. The turtle doesn't. And a barracudo could go nuts trying to eat a turtle. This would be perfect quarry for the lazy intellectual who wants a thrill. But what about adrenalin?"

Joe said nothing. Gallegher pondered, and presently seized upon some reagents and apparatus. He tried a diamond drill. He tried acids. He tried every way he could think of to rouse the blue-eyed beast. After an hour his furious curses were interrupted by a remark from the robot.

"Well, what about adrenalin?" Joe inquired ironically.

"Shut up!" Gallegher yelped. "That thing just sits there looking at me! Adren . . . what?"

"Anger as well as fear stimulates the suprarenals, you know. I suppose any human would become infuriated by continued passive resistance."

"That's right," said the sweating Gallegher, giving the creature a final kick. He turned to the couch. "Increase the nusiance quotient enough and you can substitute anger for fear. But what about that little brown animal? I'm not mad at it."

"Have a drink," Joe suggested.

"All right, I am mad at the kleptomaniacal so-and-so!

You said it moved so fast I can't see it. How can I catch it?"

"There are undoubtedly methods."

"It's as elusive as the other critter is invulnerable. Could I immobilize it by getting it drunk?"

"Metabolism."

"Burns up its fuel too fast to get drunk? Probably. But it must need a lot of food."

"Have you looked in the kitchen lately?" Joe asked.

Visions of a depleted larder filling his mind, Gallegher rose. He paused beside the blue-eyed object.

"This one hasn't got any metabolism to speak of. But it has to eat, I suppose. Still, eat what? Air? It's possible."

The doorbell sang. Gallegher moaned, "What now?" and admitted the guest. A man with a ruddy face and a belligerent expression came in, told Gallegher he was under tentative arrest, and called in the rest of his crew, who immediately began searching the house.

"Mackenzie sent you, I suppose?" Gallegher said.

"That's right. My name's Johnson. Department of Violence, Unproved. Do you want to call counsel?"

"Yes," said Gallegher, jumping at the opportunity. He used the visor to get an attorney he knew, and began outlining his troubles. But the lawyer interrupted him.

"Sorry. I'm not taking any jobs on spec. You know my rates."

"Who said anything about spec?"

"Your last check bounced yesterday. It's cash on the line this time, or no deal."

"I. . . Now wait! I've just finished a commissioned job that's paying off big. I can have the money for you—"

"When I see the color of your credits, I'll be your lawyer," the unsympathetic voice said, and the screen blanked. The detective, Johnson, tapped Gallegher on the shoulder.

"So you're overdrawn at the bank, eh? Needed money?"

"That's no secret. Besides, I'm not broke now, exactly. I finished a—"

"A job. Yeah, I heard that, too. So you're suddenly rich. How much did this job pay you? It wouldn't be fifty thousand credits, would it?"

Gallegher drew a deep breath. "I'm not saying a word," he said, and retreated to the couch, trying to ignore the Department men who were searching the lab. He needed a lawyer. He needed one bad. But he couldn't get one without money. Suppose he saw Mackenzie—

The visor put him in touch with the man. Mackenzie seemed cheerful.

"Hello," he said, "see, the police have arrived."

Gallegher said, "Listen, that job your partner gave me—I've solved your problem. I've got what you want."

"Jonas's body, you mean?" Mackenzie seemed pleased.

"No! The animals you wanted! The perfect quarry!"

"Oh. Well. Why didn't you say so sooner?"

"Get over here and call off the police!" Gallegher insisted. "I tell you, I've got your ideal Hunt animals for you!"

"I dinna ken if I can call off the bloodhounds," Mackenzie said, "but I'll be over directly. I will not pay vurra much, you understand?"

"Bah!" Gallegher snarled, and broke the connection. The visor buzzed at him. He touched the receiver, and a woman's face came in.

She said: "Mr. Gallegher, with reference to your call of inquiry regarding your grandfather, we report that investigation shows that he has not returned to our Maine sector. That is all."

She vanished. Johnson said: "What's this? Your grandfather? Where's he at?"

"I ate him," Gallegher said, twitching. "Why don't you leave me alone?"

Johnson made a note. "Your grandfather. I'll just check up a bit. Incidentally, what's that thing over there?" He pointed to the blue-eyed beast.

"I've been studying a curious case of degenerative osteomyelitis affecting a baroque cephalopod!"

"Oh, I see. Thanks. Fred, see about this guy's grandfather. What are you gaping at?"

Fred said: "That screen. It's set up for projection."

Johnson moved to the audio-sonic recorder. "Better impound it. Probably not important, but—" He touched a switch. The screen turned blank, but Gallegher's voice said: *"We know how to deal with spies in this house, you dirty traitor."*

Johnson moved the switch again. He glanced at Gallegher, his ruddy face impassive, and in silence began to rewind the wire tape. Gallegher said: "Joe, get me a dull knife. I want to cut my throat, and I don't want to make it too easy for myself. I'm getting used to doing things the hard way."

But Joe, pondering philosophy, refused to answer.

Johnson began to run off the recording. He took out a picture and compared it with what showed on the screen.

"That's Harding, all right," he said. "Thanks for keeping this for us, Mr. Gallegher."

"Don't mention it," Gallegher said. "I'll even show the hangman how to tie the knot around my neck."

"Ha-ha. Taking notes, Fred? Right."

The reel unrolled relentlessly. But, Gallegher tried to

make himself believe, there was nothing really incriminating recorded.

He was disillusioned after the screen went blank, at the point when he had thrown a blanket over the recorder last night. Johnson held up his hand for silence. The screen still showed nothing, but after a moment or two voices were clearly audible.

*"You have thirty-seven minutes to go, Mr. Gallegher."*

*"Just stay where you are. I'll have this in a minute. Besides, I want to get my hands on your fifty thousand credits."*

*"But–"*

*"Relax. I'm getting it. In a very short time your worries will be over."*

"Did I say that?" Gallegher thought wildly. "What a fool I am! Why didn't I turn off the radio when I covered up the lens?"

Grandpa's voice said: *"Trying to kill me by inches, eh, you young whippersnapper!"*

"All the old so-and-so wanted was another bottle," Gallegher moaned to himself. "But try to make those flatfeet believe that! Still—" He brightened. "Maybe I can find out what really happened to Grandpa and Harding. If I shot them off to another world, there might be some clue—"

*"Watch closely now,"* Gallegher's voice said from last night. *"I'll explain as I proceed. Oh-oh. Wait a minute. I'm going to patent this later, so I don't want any spies. I can trust you two not to talk, but that recorder's still turned on to audio. Tomorrow, if I played it back, I'd be saying to myself, 'Gallegher, you talk too much. There's only one way to keep a secret safe.' Off it goes!"*

Someone screamed. The shriek was cut off midway. The projector stopped humming. There was utter silence.

• • •

The door opened to admit Murdoch Mackenzie. He was rubbing his hands.

"I came right down," he said briskly. "So you've solved our problem, eh, Mr. Gallagher? Perhaps we can do business then. After all, there's no real evidence that you killed Jonas—and I'll be willing to drop the charges, *if* you've got what Adrenals, Incorporated, wants."

"Pass me those handcuffs, Fred." Johnson requested.

Gallegher protested, "You can't do this to me!"

"A fallacious theorem," Joe said, "which, I note, is now being disproved by the empirical method. How illogical all you ugly people are."

The social trend always lags behind the technological one. And while technology tended, in these days, toward simplification, the social pattern was immensely complicated, since it was partly an outgrowth of historical precedent and partly a result of the scientific advance of the era. Take jurisprudence. Cockburn and Blackwood and a score of others had established certain general and specific rules—say, regarding patents—but those rules could be made thoroughly impractical by a single gadget. The Integrators could solve problems no human brain could manage, so, as a governor, it was necessary to build various controls into those semimechanical colloids. Moreover, an electronic duplicator could infringe not only on patents but on property rights, and attorneys prepared voluminous briefs on such questions as whether "rarity rights" are real property, whether a gadget made on a duplicator is a "representation" or a copy, and whether mass-duplication of chinchillas is unfair competition to a chinchilla breeder who depended on old-fashioned biological principles. All of which added up to the fact that the world, slightly punch-drunk with technology, was trying desperately to walk a straight line. Eventually the confusion would settle down.

It hadn't settled down yet.

So legal machinery was a construction far more complicated than an Integrator. Precedent warred with abstract theory as lawyer warred with lawyer. It was all perfectly clear to the technicians, but they were much too impractical to be consulted; they were apt to remark wickedly, "So my gadget unstabilizes property rights? Well—why have property rights, then?"

And you can't do that!

Not to a world that had found security, of a sort, for thousands of years in rigid precedents of social intercourse. The ancient dyke of formal culture was beginning to leak in innumerable spots, and, had you noticed, you might have seen hundreds of thousands of frantic, small figures rushing from danger-spot to danger-spot, valorously plugging the leaks with their fingers, arms, or heads. Some day it would be discovered that there was no encroaching ocean beyond that dyke, but that day hadn't yet come.

In a way, that was lucky for Gallegher. Public officials were chary about sticking their necks out. A simple suit for false arrest might lead to fantastic ramifications and big trouble. The hard-headed Murdoch Mackenzie took advantage of this situation to vise his own personal attorney and toss a monkey wrench in the legal wheels. The attorney spoke to Johnson.

There was no corpse. The audiosonic recording was not sufficient. Moreover, there were vital questions involving *habeus corpus* and search warrants. Johnson called Headquarters Jurisprudence and the argument raged over the heads of Gallegher and the imperturbable Mackenzie. It ended with Johnson leaving, with his crew—and the increasing recording—and threatening to return as soon as a judge could issue the appropriate writs and papers. Meanwhile, he said, there would be officers on guard outside the house. With a malignant glare for Mackenzie, he stamped out.

"And now to business," said Mackenzie, rubbing his hands. "Between ourselves"—he leaned forward confidentially—"I'm just as glad to get rid of that partner of mine. Whether or not you killed him, I hope he stays vanished. Now I can run the business my way, for a change."

"It's all right about that," Gallegher said, "but what about me? I'll be in custody again as soon as Johnson can wangle it."

"But not convicted," Mackenzie pointed out. "A clever lawyer can fix you up. There was a similar case in which the defendant got off with a defense of *non esse*—his attorney went into metaphysics and proved that the murdered man had never existed. Quite specious, but so far the murderer's gone free."

Gallegher said: "I've searched the house, and Johnson's men did, too. There's simply no trace of Jonas Harding or my grandfather. And I'll tell you frankly, Mr. Mackenzie, I haven't the slightest idea what happened to them."

Mackenzie gestured airily. "We must be methodical. You mentioned you had solved a certain problem for Adrenals, Incorporated. Now, I'll admit, that interested me."

Silently Gallegher pointed to the blue-eyed dynamo. Mackenzie studied the object thoughtfully.

"Well?" he said.

"That's it. The perfect quarry."

Mackenzie walked over to the thing, rapped its hide,

and looked deeply into the mild azure eyes. "How fast can it run?" he asked shrewdly.

Gallegher said: "It doesn't have to run. You see, it's invulnerable."

"Ha. Hum. Perhaps if you'd explain a wee bit more—"

But Mackenzie did not seem pleased with the explanation. "No," he said, "I don't see it. There would be no thrill to hunting a critter like that. You forget our customers demand excitement—adrenal stimulation."

"They'll get it. Anger has the same effect as rage—" Gallegher went into detail.

But Mackenzie shook his head. "Both fear and anger

give you excess energy you've got to use up. You can't, against a passive quarry. You'll just cause neuroses. We try to get rid of neuroses, not create them."

Gallegher, growing desperate, suddenly remembered the little brown beast and began to discuss that. Once, Mackenzie interrupted with a demand to see the creature. Gallegher slid around that one fast.

"Ha," Mackenzie said finally. "It isna canny. How can you hunt something that's invisible?"

"Oh—ultraviolet. Scent-analyzers. It's a test for ingenuity—"

"Our customers are not ingenious. They don't want to be. They want a change and a vacation from routine, hard work—or easy work, as the case may be—they want a rest. They don't want to beat their brains working out methods to catch a thing that moves faster than a pixy, nor do they want to chase a critter that's out of sight before it even gets there. You are a vurra clever man, Mr. Gallegher, but it begins to look as though Jonas's insurance is my best bet after all."

"Now wait—"

Mackenzie pursed his lips. "I'll admit the beasties *may*—I say may—have some possibilities. But what good is quarry that can't be caught? Perhaps if you'd work out a way to capture these other—worldly animals of yours, we might do business. At present, I willna buy a pig in a poke."

"I'll find a way," Gallegher promised wildly. "But I can't do it in jail."

"Ah. I am a little irritated with you, Mr. Gallegher. You tricked me into believing you had solved our problem. Which you havena done—yet. Consider the thought of jail. Your adrenalin may stimulate your brain into working out a way to trap these animals of yours. Though, even so, I can make no rash promises—"

Murdoch Mackenzie grinned at Gallegher and went out, closing the door softly behind him. Gallegher began to dine off his finger nails.

"Men can know the nature of things," Joe said, with an air of solid conviction.

At that point matters were complicated even further by the appearance, on the televisor screen, of a gray-haired man who announced that one of Gallegher's checks had just bounced. Three hundred and fifty credits, the man said, and how about it?

Gallegher looked dazedly at the identification card on the screen. "You're with United Cultures? What's that?"

The gray-haired man said silkily, "Biological and medical supplies and laboratories, Mr. Gallegher."

"What did I order from you?"

"We have a receipt for six hundred pounds of Vitaplasm, first grade. We made delivery within an hour."

"And when—"

The gray-haired man went into more detail. Finally Gallegher made a few lying promises and turned from the blanking screen. He looked wildly around the lab.

"Six hundred pounds of artificial protoplasm," he murmured. "Ordered by Gallegher Plus. He's got delusions of economic grandeur."

"It was delivered," Joe said. "You signed the receipt, the night Grandpa and Jonas Harding disappeared."

"But what could I do with the stuff? It's used for plastic surgery and for humano-prosthesis. Artificial limbs and stuff. It's cultured cellular tissue, this Vitaplasm. Did I use it to *make* some animals? That's biologically impossible. I think. How could I have molded Vitaplasm into a little brown animal that's invisible? What about the brain and the neural structure? Joe, six hundred pounds of Vitaplasm has simply disappeared. Where has it gone?"

But Joe was silent.

Hours later Gallegher was furiously busy. "The trick is," he explained to Joe, "to find out all I can about those critters. Then maybe I can tell where they came from and how I got 'em. Then perhaps I can discover where Grandpa and Harding went. Then—"

"Why not sit down and think about it?"

"That's the difference between us. You've got no instinct of self-preservation. You could sit down and think while a chain reaction took place in your toes and worked up, but not me. I'm too young to die. I keep thinking of Reading Gaol. I need a drink. If I could only get high, my demon subconscious could work out the whole problem for me. Is that little brown animal around?"

"No," Joe said.

"Then maybe I can steal a drink." Gallegher exploded, after an abortive attempt that ended in utter failure: "Nobody can move *that* fast."

"Accelerated metabolism. It must have smelled alcohol. Or perhaps it has additional senses. Even I can scarcely varish it."

"If I mixed kerosene with the whisky, maybe the dipsomaniacal little monster would't like it. Still, neither would I. Ah, well. Back to the mill," Gallegher said, as he tried reagent after reagent on the blue-eyed dynamo, without any effect at all.

"Men can know the nature of things." Joe said irritatingly.

"Shut up. I wonder if I could electroplate this creature? That would immobilize it, all right. But it's immobilized already. How does it eat?"

"Logically, I'd say osmosis."

"Very likely. Osmosis of what?"

Joe clicked irritatedly. "There are dozens of ways you could solve your problem. Instrumentalism. Determinism. Vitalism. Work from *a posteriori to a priori*. It's perfectly obvious to me that you've solved the problem Adrenals, Incorporated, set you."

"I have?"

"Certainly."

"How?"

"Very simple. Men can know the nature of things."

"Will you stop repeating that out-moded basic and try to be useful? You're wrong, anyway. Men can know the nature of things by experiment and reason combined!"

Joe said: "Ridiculous. Philosophical incompetence. If you can't prove your point by logic, you've failed. Anybody who has to depend on experiment is beneath contempt."

"Why should I sit here arguing philosophical concepts with a robot?" Gallegher demanded of no one in particular. "How would you like me to demonstrate the fact that ideation is dependent on your having a radioatomic brain that isn't scattered all over the floor?"

"Kill me, then," Joe said. "It's your loss and the world's. Earth will be a poorer place when I die. But coercion means nothing to me. I have no instinct of self-preservation."

"Now look," Gallegher said, trying a new tack, "if you know the answer, why not tell me? Demonstrate that wonderful logic of yours. Convince me without having to depend on experiment. Use pure reason."

"Why should I want to convince you? *I'm* convinced. And I'm so beautiful and perfect that I can achieve no higher glory than to admire me."

"Narcissus," Gallegher snarled. "You're a combination of Narcissus and Nietzsche's Superman."

"Men can know the nature of things," Joe said.

The next development was a subpoena for the transparent robot. The legal machinery was beginning to move, an immensely complicated gadget that worked on a logic as apparently twisted as Joe's own. Gallegher himself, it seemed, was temporarily inviolate, through some odd interpretation of jurisprudence. But the State's principle was that the sum of the parts was equal to the whole. Joe was classified as one of the parts, the total of which equaled Gallegher. Thus the robot found itself in court, listening to a polemic with impassive scorn.

Gallegher, flanked by Murdoch Mackenzie and a corps of attorneys, was with Joe. This was an informal hearing. Gallegher didn't pay much attention; he was concentrating on finding a way to put the bite on the recalcitrant robot, who knew all the answers but wouldn't talk. He had been studying the philosophers, with an eye toward meeting Joe on his own ground, but so far had succeeded only in acquiring a headache and an almost unendurable longing for a drink. Even out of his laboratory, though, he remained Tantalus. The invisible little brown animal followed him around and stole his liquor.

One of Mackenzie's lawyers jumped up. "I object," he said. There was a brief wrangle as to whether Joe should be classified as a witness or as Exhibit A. If the latter, the subpoena had been falsely served. The Justice pondered.

"As I see it," he declared, "the question is one of determinism versus voluntarism. If this . . . ah . . . robot has free will—"

"Ha!" Gallegher said, and was shushed by an attorney. He subsided rebelliously.

"—then it, or he, is a witness. But, on the other hand, there is the possibility that the robot, in acts of apparent choice, is the mechanical expression of heredity and past environment. For heredity read . . . ah . . . initial mechanical basics."

"Whether or not the robot is a rational being, Mr. Justice, is beside the point," the prosecutor put in.

"I do not agree. Law is based on *res*–"

Joe said: "Mr. Justice, may I speak?"

"Your ability to do so rather automatically gives you permission," the Justice said, studying the robot in a baffled way. "Go ahead."

Joe had seemingly found the connection between law, logic, and philosophy. He said happily: "I've figured it all out. A thinking robot is a rational being. I am a thinking robot—therefore I am a rational being."

"What a fool," Gallegher groaned, longing for the sane logics or electronics and chemistry. "The old Socratic syllogism. Even I could point out the flaw in that?"

"Quiet," Mackenzie whispered. "All the lawyers really depend on is tying up the case in such knots nobody can figure it out. Your robot is perhaps not such a fool as you think."

An argument started as to whether thinking robots really were rational beings. Gallegher brooded. He couldn't see the point, really. Nor did it become clear until, from the maze of contradictions, there emerged the tentative decision that Joe was a rational being. This seemed to please the prosecutor immensely.

"Mr. Justice," he announced, "we have learned that Mr. Galloway Gallegher two nights ago inactivated the robot before us now. Is this not true, Mr. Gallegher?"

But Mackenzie's hand kept Gallegher in his seat. One of the defending attorneys rose to meet the question.

"We admit nothing," he said. "However, if you wish to pose a theoretical question, we will answer it."

The query was posed theoretically.

"Then the theoretical answer is 'yes,' Mr. Prosecutor. A robot of this type can be turned on and off at will."

"Can the robot turn itself off?"

"Yes."

"But this did not occur? Mr. Gallegher inactivated the robot at the time Mr. Jonas Harding was with him in his laboratory two nights ago?"

"Theoretically, that is true. There was a temporary inactivation."

"Then," said the prosecutor, "we wish to question the robot, who has been classed as a rational being."

"The decision was tentative," the defense objected.

"Accepted. Mr. Justice—"

"All right," said the Justice, who was still staring at Joe, "you may ask your questions."

"Ah... ah—" The prosecutor, facing the robot, hesitated.

"Call me Joe," Joe said.

"Thank you. Ah... is this true? Did Mr. Gallegher inactivate you at the time and place stated?"

"Yes."

"Then," the prosecutor said triumphantly, "I wish to bring a charge of assault and battery against Mr. Gallegher. Since this robot has been tentatively classed as a rational being, any activity causing him, or it, to lose consciousness or the power of mobility is *contra bonos mores,* and may be classed as mayhem."

Mackenzie's attorneys were ruffled. Gallegher said: "What does that mean?"

A lawyer whispered: "They can hold you, and hold that robot as a witness." He stood up. "Mr. Justice. Our statements were in reply to purely theoretical questions."

The prosecutor said: "But the robot's statement answered a non-theoretical question."

"The robot was not on oath."

"Easily remedied," said the prosecutor, while Gallegher saw his last hopes slipping rapidly away. He thought hard, while matters proceeded.

"Do you solemnly swear to tell the truth the whole truth and nothing but the truth so help you God?"

Gallegher leaped to his feet. "Mr. Justice, I object."

"Indeed. To what?"

"To the validity of that oath."

Mackenzie said: "Ah- *ha!*"

The Justice was thoughtful. "Will you please elucidate, Mr. Gallegher? Why should the oath not be administered to this robot?"

"Such an oath is applicable to man only."

"And?"

"It presupposes the existence of the soul. At least it implies theism, a personal religion. Can a robot take an oath?"

The Justice eyed Joe. "It's a point, certainly. Ah. . . Joe. Do you believe in a personal deity?"

"I do."

The prosecutor beamed. "Then we can proceed."

"Wait a minute," Murdoch Mackenzie said, rising. "May I ask a question, Mr. Justice?"

"Go ahead."

Mackenzie stared at the robot. "Well, now. Will you tell me, please, what this personal deity of yours is like?"

"Certainly," Joe said. "Just like me."

After a while it degenerated into a theological argument. Gallegher left the attorneys debating the apparently vital point of how many angels could dance on the head of a pin, and went home temporarily scot-free, with Joe. Until such points as the robot's religious basics were settled, nothing could be done. All the way, in the aircab, Mackenzie insisted on pointing out the merits of Calvinism to Joe.

At the door Mackenzie made a mild threat. "I did not intend to give you so much rope, you understand. But you will work all the harder with the threat of prison hanging over your head. I don't know how long I can keep you a free man. If you can work out an answer quickly— "

"What sort of answer?"

"I am easily satisfied. Jonas's body, now— "

"Bah!" Gallegher said, and went into his laboratory and sat down morosely. He siphoned himself a drink before he remembered the little brown animal. Then he lay back, staring from the blue-eyed dynamo to Joe and back again.

Finally he said: "There's an old Chinese idea that the man who first stops arguing and starts swinging with his fists admits his intellectual defeat."

Joe said: "Naturally. Reason is sufficient; if you need experiment to prove your point, you're a lousy philosopher and logician."

Gallegher fell back on casuistry. "First step, animal. Fist-swinging. Second step, human. Pure logic. But what about the third step?"

"What third step?"

"Men can know the nature of things —but you're not a man. Your personal deity isn't an anthropomorphic one. Three steps: animal, man, and what we'll call for convenience, superman—though *man* doesn't necessarily enter into it. We've always attributed godlike traits to the theoretical superbeing. Suppose, just for the sake of having a label, we call this third-stage entity Joe."

"Why not?" Joe said.

"Then the two basic concepts of logic don't apply. Men can know the nature of things by pure reason, and also by experiment *and* reason. But such second-stage concepts are as elementary to Joe as Plato's ideas were to Aristotle." Gallegher crossed his fingers behind his back. "The question is, then, what's the third-stage operation for Joe?"

"Godlike?" the robot said.

"You've got special senses, you know. You can varish, whatever that is. Do you need ordinary logical methods? Suppose—"

"Yes," Joe said, "I can varish, all right. I can skren, too. Hm-m-m."

Gallegher abruptly rose from the couch. "What a fool I am. 'DRINK ME'. That's the answer. Joe, shut up. Go off in a corner and varish."

"I'm skrenning," Joe said.

"Then skren. I've finally got an idea. When I woke up yesterday, I was thinking about a bottle labeled 'DRINK ME'. When Alice took a drink, she changed size, didn't she? Where's that reference book? I wish I knew more about technology. Vasoconstrictor...hemostatic...here it is—demonstrates the metabolic regulation mechanisms of the vegetative nervous system. Metabolism. I wonder now—"

Gallegher rushed to the workbench and examined the bottles. "Vitalism. Life is the basic reality, of which everything else is a form or manifestation. Now. I had a problem to solve for Adrenals, Incorporated. Jonas Harding and Grandpa were here. Harding gave me an hour to fill the bill. The problem...a dangerous and harmless animal. Paradox. That isn't it. Harding's clients wanted thrills and safety at the same time. I've got no lab animals on tap at the moment... *Joe!*"

"Well?"

"Watch," Gallegher said. He poured a drink and watched the liquid vanish before he tasted it. "Now. What happened?"

"The little brown animal drank it."

"Is that little brown animal, by any chance—Grandpa?"

"That's right," Joe said.

Gallegher blistered the robot's transparent hide with sulphurous oaths. "Why didn't you tell me? You—"

"I answered your question," the robot said smugly. "Grandpa's brown, isn't he? And he's an animal."

"But—little! I thought it was a critter about as big as a rabbit."

"The only standard of comparison is the majority of the species. That's the yardstick. Compared to the average height of humans, Grandpa *is* little. A little brown animal."

"So it's Grandpa, is it?" Gallegher said, returning to the workbench. "And he's simply speeded up. Accelerated metabolism. Adrenalin. Hm-m-m. Now I know what to look for, maybe—"

He fell to. But it was sundown before Gallegher emptied a small vial into a glass, siphoned whisky into it, and watched the mixture disappear.

A flickering began. Something flashed from corner to corner of the room. Gradually it became visible as a streaking brownness that resolved itself, finally, into Grandpa. He stood before Gallegher, jittering like mad as the last traces of the accelerative formula wore off.

"Hello, Grandpa," Gallegher said placatingly.

Grandpa's nutcracker face wore an expression of malevolent fury. For the first time in his life, the old gentleman was drunk. Gallegher stared in utter amazement.

"I'm going back to Maine," Grandpa cried, and fell over backwards.

• • •

"Never seen such a lot of slow pokes in my life," Grandpa said, devouring a steak. "My, I'm hungry. Next time I let you stick a needle in me I'll know better. How many months have I been like this?"

"Two days," Gallegher said, carefully mixing up a formula. "It was a metabolic accelerator, Grandpa. You just lived faster, that's all."

"All! Bah. Couldn't eat nothing. Food was solid as a rock. Only thing I could get down my gullet was liquor."

"Oh?"

"Hard chewing. Even with my store teeth. Even whisky tasted hotter. As for a steak like this, I couldn't've managed it."

"You were living faster." Gallegher glanced at the robot, who was still quietly skrenning in a corner. "Let me see. The antithesis of an accelerator is a decelerator—Grandpa, where's Jonas Harding?"

"In there," Grandpa said, pointing to the blue-eyed dynamo and thus confirming Gallegher's suspicion.

"Vitaplasm. So that was it. That's why I had a lot of Vitaplasm sent over a couple of nights ago. Hm-m-m." Gallegher examined the sleek, impermeable surface of the apparent dynamo. After a while he tried a hypodermic syringe. He couldn't penetrate the hard shell.

Instead, using a new mixture he had concocted from the bottles on his workbench, he dripped a drop of the liquid on the substance. Presently it softened. At that spot Gallegher made an injection, and was delighted to see a color-change spread out from the locus till the entire mass was pallid and plastic.

"Vitaplasm," he exulted. "Ordinary artificial protoplasm cells, that's all. No wonder it looked hard. I'd given it a decelerative treatment. An approach to molecular stasis. Anything metabolizing that slowly would seem hard as iron." He wadded up great bunches of the surrogate and dumped it into a convenient vat. Something began to form around the blue eyes—the shape of a cranium, broad shoulders, a torso—

Freed from the disguising mass of Vitaplasm, Jonas Harding was revealed crouching on the floor, silent as a statue.

His heart wasn't beating. He didn't breathe. The decelerator held him in an unbreakable grip of passivity.

Not quite unbreakable. Gallegher, about to apply the hypodermic, paused and looked from Joe to Grandpa. "Now why did I do that?" he demanded.

Then he answered his own question.

"The time limit. Harding gave me an hour to solve his problem. Time's relative—especially when your metabolism is slowed down. I must have given Harding a shot of the decelerator so he wouldn't realize how much time had passed. Let's see." Gallegher applied a drop to Harding's impermeable skin and watched the spot soften and change hue. "Uh-huh. With Harding frozen like that, I could take weeks to work on the problem, and when he woke up, he'd figure only a short time had passed. But why did I use the Vitaplasm on him?"

Grandpa downed a beer. "When you're drunk, you're apt to do anything," he contended, reaching for another steak.

"True, true. But Gallegher Plus is logical. A strange, eerie kind of logic, but logic nevertheless. Let me see. I shot the decelerator into Harding, and then—there he was. Rigid and stiff. I couldn't leave him kicking around the lab, could I?

If anybody came in they'd think I had a corpse on my hands!"

"You mean he ain't dead?" Grandpa demanded.

"Of course not. Merely decelerated. I know! I camouflaged Harding's body. I sent out for Vitaplasm, molded the stuff around his body, and then applied the decelerator to the Vitaplasm. It works on living cellular substance—slows it down. And slowed down to that extent, it's impermeable and immovable!"

"You're crazy," Grandpa said.

"I'm short-sighted," Gallegher admitted. "At least, Gallegher Plus is. Imagine leaving Harding's eyes visible, so I'd be reminded the guy was under that pile when I woke up from my binge! What did I construct that recorder for, anyhow? The logic Gallegher Plus uses is far more fantastic than Joe's."

"Don't bother me," Joe said. "I'm still skrenning."

Gallegher put the hypodermic needle into the soft spot on Harding's arm. He injected the accelerator, and within a moment or two Jonas Harding stirred, blinked his blue eyes, and got up from the floor. "Ouch!" he said, rubbing his arm. "Did you stick me with something?"

"An accident," Gallegher said, watching the man warily. "Uh . . . this problem of yours—"

Harding found a chair and sat down, yawning. "Solved it?"

"You gave me an hour."

"Oh. Yes, of course." Harding looked at his watch. "It's stopped. Well, what about it?"

"Just how long a time do you think has lapsed since you came into this laboratory?"

"Half an hour?" Harding hazarded.

"Two months," Grandpa snapped.

"You're both right," Gallegher said. "I'd have another answer, but I'd be right, too."

Harding obviously thought that Gallegher was still drunk. He stayed doggedly on the subject.

"What about that specialized animal we need? You still have half an hour—"

"I don't need it," Gallegher said, a great white light dawning in his mind. "I've got your answer for you. But it isn't quite what you think it is." He relaxed on the couch and considered the liquor-organ. Now that he could drink again, he found he preferred to prolong the anticipation.

"I came upon no wine so wonderful as thirst," he remarked.

"Claptrap," Grandpa said.

Gallegher said: "The clients of Adrenals, Incorporated, want to hunt animals. They want a thrill, so they need dangerous animals. They have to be safe, so they can't have dangerous animals. It seems paradoxical, but it isn't. The answer doesn't lie in the animal. It's in the hunter."

Harding blinked. "Come again?"

"Tigers. Ferocious man-eating tigers. Lions. Jaguars. Water buffalo. The most vicious, carnivorous animals you can get. That's part of the answer."

"Listen—" Harding said. "Maybe you've got the wrong idea. The tigers aren't our customers. We don't supply clients to the animals, it's the other way round."

"I must make a few more tests," Gallegher said, "but the basic priciple's right here in my hand. An accelerator. A latent metabolic accelerator with a strong concentration of adrenalin as the catalyst. Like this—"

He sketched a vivid verbal picture.

Armed with a rifle, the client wandered through the artificial jungle, seeking quarry. He had already paid his fee to Adrenals, Incorporated, and got his intravenous shot of the latent accelerator. That substance permeated his blood stream, doing nothing as yet, waiting for the catalyst.

The tiger launched itself from the underbrush. It shot toward the client like catapulted murder, fangs bared. As the claws neared the man's back, the suprarenals shot adrenalin into the blood stream in strong concentration.

That was the catalyst. The latent accelerative factor became active.

The client speeded up —tremendously.

He stepped away from the body of the tiger, apparently frozen in midair, and did what seemed best to him before the effect of the accelerator wore off. When it did, he returned to normal—and by that time he could be in the supply station of Adrenals, Incorporated, getting another intravenous shot—unless he'd decided to bag his tiger the easy way.

It was as simple as that.

"Ten thousand credits," Gallegher said, happily counting them. "The balance due as soon as I work out the catalytic angle. Which is a cinch. Any fourth-rate chemist could do it. What intrigues me is the forthcoming interview between Harding and Murdoch Mackenzie. When they compare the time element, it's going to be funny."

"I want a drink," Grandpa said. "Where's a bottle?"

"Even in court, I think I could prove I only took an hour or less to solve the problem. It was Harding's hour, of course, but time *is* relative. Entropy—metabolism—what a legal battle *that* would be! Still, it won't happen. I know the formula for the accelerator and Harding doesn't. He'll pay the other forty thousand—and Mackenzie won't have any kicks. After all, I'm giving Adrenals, Incorporated, the success factor they needed."

"Well, I'm still going back to Maine," Grandpa contended. "Least you can do is give me a bottle."

"Go out and buy one," Gallegher said, tossing the old gentleman several credits. "Buy several. I often wonder what the vintners buy—"

"Eh?"

" —one-half so precious as the stuff they sell. No, I'm not tight. But I'm going to be." Gallegher clutched the liquor-organ's mouth-piece in a loving grip and began to play alcoholic arpeggios on the keyboard. Grandpa, with a parting sneer at such new-fangled contraptions, took his departure.

Silence fell over the laboratory. Bubbles and Monstro, the two dynamos, sat quiescent. Neither of them had bright blue eyes. Gallegher experimented with cocktails and felt a warm, pleasant glow seep through his soul.

Joe came out of his corner and stood before the mirror, admiring his gears.

"Finished skrenning?" Gallegher asked sardonically.

"Yes."

"Rational being, forsooth. You and your philosophy. Well, my fine robot, it turned out I didn't need your help after all. Pose away."

"How ungrateful you are," Joe said, "after I've given you the benefit of my superlogic."

"Your...what? You've slipped a gear. What superlogic?"

"The third-stage, of course. What we were talking

about a while back. That's why I was skrenning. I hope you didn't think all your problems were solved by your feeble brain, in that opaque cranium of yours."

Gallegher sat up. "What are your talking about? Third-stage logic? You didn't—"

"I don't think I can describe it to you. It's more abstruse than the noumenon of Kant, which can't be perceived except by thought. You've got to be able to skren to understand it, but—well, it's the third stage. It's... let's see... demonstrating the nature of things by making things happen by themselves."

"Experiment?"

"No. By skrenning, I reduce all things from the material plane to the realm of pure thought, and figure out the logical concepts and solutions."

"But... wait. Things have been *happening!* I figured out about Grandpa and Harding and worked out the accelerator—"

"You think you did," Joe said. "I simply skrenned. Which is a purely superintellectual process. After I'd done that, things couldn't help happening. But I hope you don't think they happened by themselves!"

Gallegher said: "What's skrenning?"

"You'll never know."

"But... you're contending you're the First Cause... no, it's voluntarism... third-stage logic? No—" Gallegher fell back on the couch, staring. "Who do you think you are? *Deus ex machina?*"

Joe glanced down at the conglomeration of gears in his torso.

"What else?" he asked smugly.

He discovered the secret immortality—and a way to escape forever the boredom that never-ending life would eventually, inevitably, mean. But he never knew that latter fact.

# Invariant

**By John Pierce**
Illustrated by Williams

You know the general facts concerning Homer Green, so I don't need to describe him or his surroundings. I knew as much and more, yet it was an odd sensation, which you don't get through reading, actually to dress in that primitive fashion, to go among strange surroundings, and to see him.

The house is no more odd than the pictures. Hemmed in by other twentieth century buildings, it must be indistinguishable from the original structure and its surroundings. To enter it, to tread on rugs, to see chairs covered in cloth with a nap, to see instruments for smoking, to see and hear a primitive radio, even though operating really from a variety of authentic transcriptions, and above all, to see an open fire; all this gave me a sense of unreality, prepared though I was. Green sat by the fire in a chair, as we almost invariably find him, with a dog at his feet. He is perhaps the most valuable man in the world, I thought. But I could not shake off the sense of unreality concerning the substantial surroundings. He, too, seemed unreal, and I pitied him.

The sense of unreality continued through the form of

self-introduction. How many have there been! I could, of course, examine the records.

I'm Carew, from the Institute," I said. "We haven't met before, but they told me you'd be glad to see me."

Green rose and extended his hand. I took it obediently, making the unfamiliar gesture.

"Glad to see you," he said. "I've been dozing here. It's a little of a shock, the treatment, and I thought I'd rest a few days. I hope it's really permanent.

"Won't you sit down?" he added.

We seated ourselves before the fire. The dog, which had risen, lay down, pressed against his master's feet.

"I suppose you want to test my reactions?" Green asked.

"Later," I replied. "There's no hurry. And it's so very comfortable here."

Green was easily distracted. He relaxed, staring at the fire. This was an opportunity, and I spoke in a somewhat purposeful voice.

"It seems more a time for politics, here," I said. "What the Swede intends, and what the French—"

"Drench our thoughts in mirth—" Green replied.

I had thought from the records the quotation would have some effect.

"But one doesn't leave politics to drench his thoughts in mirth," he continued. "One studies them—"

I won't go into the conversation. You've seen it in Appendix A of my thesis, "An Aspect of Twentieth Century Politics and Speech." It was brief, as you know. I had been very lucky to get to see Green. I was more lucky to hit on the right thread directly. Somehow, it had never occurred to me before that twentieth century politicians had meant, or had thought that they meant, what they said; that indeed, they had in their own minds attached a sense of meaning or relevancy to what seem to us meaningless or irrelevant phrases. It's hard to explain so foreign an idea; perhaps an example would help.

For instance, would you believe that a man accused of making a certain statement would seriously reply, "I'm not in the habit of making such statements?" Would you believe that this might even mean that he had not made the statement? Or would you further believe that even if he had made the statement, this would seem to him to classify it as some sort of special instance, and his reply as not truly evasive? I think these conjectures plausible, that is, when I struggle to immerse myself in the twentieth century. But I would never have dreamed them before talking with Green. How truly invaluable the man is!

I have said that the conversation recorded in Appendix A is very short. There was no need to continue along political lines after I had grasped the basic idea. Twentieth century records are much more complete than Green's memory, and that itself has been thoroughly catalogued. It is not the airy bones of information, but the personal contact, the infinite variation in combinations, the stimulation of the warm human touch, that are helpful and suggestive.

So I was with Green, and most of a morning was still before me. You know that he is given meal times free, and only one appointment between meals, so that there will be no overlapping. I was grateful to the man, and sympathetic, and I was somewhat upset in his presence. I wanted to talk to him of the thing nearest his heart. There was no reason I shouldn't. I've recorded the rest of the conversation, but not published it. It's not new. Perhaps it is trivial, but it means a great deal to me. Maybe it's only my very personal memory of it. But I thought you might like to know.

"What led to your discovery?" I asked him.

"Salamanders," he replied without hesitation. "Salamanders."

The account I got of his perfect regeneration experiments was, of course, the published story. How many thousands of times has it been told? Yet, I swear I detected variations from the records. How nearly infinite the possible combinations are! But the chief points came in the usual order. How the regeneration of limbs in salamanders led to the idea of perfect regeneration of human parts. How, say, a cut heals, leaving not a scar, but a perfect replica of the damaged tissue. How in normal metabolism tissue can be replaced not imperfectly, as in an aging organism, but perfectly, indefinitely. You've seen it in animals, in compulsory biology. The chick whose metabolism replaces its tissues, but always in an exact, invariant form, never changing. It's disturbing to think of it in a man. Green looked so young, as young as I. Since the twentieth century—

When Green had concluded his description, including that of his own innoculation in the evening, he ventured to prophesy.

"I feel confident," he said, "that it will work, indefinitely."

"It does work, Dr. Green," I assured him. "Indefinitely."

"We mustn't be premature," he said. "After all, a short time—"

"Do you recall the date, Dr. Green?" I asked.

"September, 11th," he said. "1943."

"Dr. Green, today is August 4, 2170," I told him earnestly.

"Look here," Green said. "If it were, I wouldn't be here dressed this way, and you wouldn't be there dressed that way."

The impasse could have continued indefinitely. I took my communicator from my pocket and showed it to him. He watched with growing wonder and delight as I demonstrated, finally with projection, binaural and stereo. Not simple, but exactly the sort of electronic development which a man of Green's era associated with the future. Green seemed to have lost all thought of the conversation which had led to my production of the communicator.

"Dr. Green," I said, "the year is 2170. This is the twenty-second century."

He looked at me baffled, but this time not with disbelief. A strange sort of terror was spread over his features.

"An accident?" he asked. "My memory?"

"There has been no accident," I said. "Your memory is intact, as far as it goes. Listen to me. Concentrate."

Then I told him, simply and briefly, so that his thought processes would not lag. As I spoke to him he stared at me apprehensively, his mind apparently racing. This is what I said:

"Your experiment succeeded, beyond anything you had reason to hope. Your tissues took on the ability to reform themselves in exactly the same pattern year after year. Their form became invariant.

"Photographs and careful measurements show this, from year to year, yes, from century to century. You are just as you were over two hundred years ago.

"Your life has not been devoid of accident. Minor, even

major wounds have left no trace in healing. Your tissues are invariant.

"Your brain is invariant, too; that is as far as the cell patterns are concerned. A brain may be likened to an electrical network. Memory is the network, the coils and condensers, and their interconnections. Conscious thought is the pattern of voltages accross them and currents flowing through them. The pattern is complicated, but transitory—transient. Memory is changing the network of the brain, affecting all subsequent thoughts, or patterns in the network. The network of your brain never changes. It is invariant.

"Or thought is like the complicated operation of the relays and switches of a telephone exchange of your century, but memory is the interconnections of elements. The interconnections on other people's brains change in the process of thought, breaking down, building up, giving them new memories. The pattern of connections in your brain never changes. It is invariant.

"Other people can adapt themselves to new surroundings, learning where objects of necessity are, the pattern of rooms, adapting themselves unconsciously, without friction. You cannot; your brain is invariant. Your habits are keyed to a house, your house as it was the day before you treated yourself. It has been preserved, replaced through two hundred years so that you could live without friction. In it, you live, day after day, the day after the treatment which made your brain invariant.

"Do not think you give no return for this care. You are perhaps the most valuable man in the world. Morning, afternoon, evening; you have three appointments a day, when the lucky few who are judged to merit or need your help are allowed to seek it.

"I am a student of history. I came to see the twentieth century through the eyes of an intelligent man of that century. You are a very intelligent, brilliant man. Your mind has been analyzed in a detail greater than that of any other. Few brains are better. I came to learn from this powerful observant brain what politics meant to a man of your period. I learned from a fresh new source, your brain, which is not overlaid, not changed by the intervening years, but is just as it was in 1943.

"But I am not very important. Important workers: psychologists, come to see you. They ask you questions, then repeat them a little differently, and observe your reactions. One experiement is not vitiated by your memory of an earlier experiment. When your train of thought is interrupted, it leaves no memory behind. Your brain remains invariant. And these men, who otherwise could draw only general conclusions from simple experiments on multitudes of different, differently constituted and differently prepared individuals, can observe undisputable differences of response due to the slightest changes in stimulus. Some of these men have driven you to a frenzy. You do not go mad. Your brain cannot change; it is invariant.

"You are so valuable it seems that the world could scarcely progress without your invariant brain. And yet, we have not asked another to do as you did. With animals, yes. Your dog is an example. What you did was willingly, and you did not know the consequences. You did the world this greatest service unknowingly. But we know."

Green's head had sunk to his chest. His face was troubled, and he seemed to seek solace in the warmth of the fire. The dog at his feet stirred, and he looked down, a sudden smile on his face. I knew that his train of thought had been interrupted. The transients had died from his brain. Our whole meeting was gone from his processes of thought.

I rose and stole away before he looked up. Perhaps I wasted the remaining hour of the morning.

Hunting down the beast, under the best of circumstances, was dangerous. But in this little police operation, the conditions required the use of inadequate means!

# Police Operation

**By H. Beam Piper**
Illustrated by Cartler

*"... there may be something in the nature of an occult police force, which operates to divert human suspicions, and to supply explanations that are good enough for whatever, somewhat in the nature of minds, human beings have–or that, if there be occult mischief makers and occult ravagers, they may be of a world also of other beings that are acting to check them, and to explain them, not benevolently, but to divert suspicion from themselves, because they, too, may be exploiting life upon this earth, but in ways more subtle, and in orderly, or organized, fashion."*

*Charles Fort:* "LO!"

## POLICE OPERATION

John Strawmyer stood, an irate figure in faded overalls and sweatwhitened black shirt, apart from the others, his back to the weathered farm-buildings and the line of yellowing woods and the cirrus-streaked blue October sky. He thrust out a work-gnarled hand accusingly.

"That there heifer was worth two hund'red, two hund'red an' fifty dollars!" he clamored. "An' that there dog was just one uh the fam'ly. An' now look at'm! I don't like t' use profane language, but you'ns gotta *do* some'n about this!"

Steve Parker, the district game protector, aimed his Leica at the carcass of the dog and snapped the shutter. "We're doing something about it," he said shortly. Then he stepped ten feet to the left and edged around the mangled heifer, choosing an angle for his camera shot.

The two men in the gray whipcords of the State police, seeing that Parker was through with the dog, moved in and squatted to examine it. The one with the triple chevrons on his sleeves took it by both forefeet and flipped it over on its back. It had been a big brute, of nondescript breed, with a rough black-and-brown coat. Something had clawed it deeply about the head, its throat was slashed transversely several times, and it had been disemboweled by a single slash that had opened its belly from breastbone to tail. They looked at it carefully, and then went to stand beside Parker while he photographed the dead heifer. Like the dog, it had been talon-raked on either side of the head, and its throat had been slashed deeply several times. In addition, flesh had been torn from one flank in great strips.

"I can't kill a bear outa season, no!" Strawmyer continued his plaint. "But a bear comes an' kills my stock an' my dog; that there's all right! That's the kinda deal a farmer always gits, in this state! I don't like t' use profane language—"

"Then don't!" Parker barked at him, impatiently. "Don't use any kind of language. Just put in your claim and shut up!" He turned to the men in whipcords and gray Stetsons. "You boys seen everything?" he asked. "Then let's go."

They walked briskly back to the barnyard, Strawmyer following them, still vociferating about the wrongs of the farmer at the hands of a cynical and corrupt State government. They climbed into the State police car, the sergeant and the private in front and Parker into the rear, laying his camera on the seat beside a Winchester carbine.

"Weren't you pretty short with that fellow back there, Steve?" the sergeant asked as the private started the car.

"Not too short. 'I don't like t' use profane language'," Parker mimicked the bereaved heifer owner, and then he went on to specify: "I'm morally certain that he's shot at least four illegal deer in the last year. When and if I ever get anything on him, he's going to be sorrier for himself then he is now."

"They're the characters that always beef their heads off," the sergeant agreed. "You think that whatever did this was the same as the others?"

"Yes. The dog must have jumped it while it was eating at the heifer. Same superficial scratches about the head, and deep cuts on the throat or belly. The bigger the animal, the farther front the big slashes occur. Evidently something grabs them by the head with front claws, and slashes with hind claws; that's why I think it's a bobcat."

"You know," the private said, "I saw a lot of wounds like that during the war. My outfit landed on Mindanao, where the guerrillas had been active. And this looks like bolo-work to me."

"The surplus-stores are full of machetes and jungle knives," the sergeant considered. "I think I'll call up Doc Winters, at the County Hospital, and see if all his squirrel-fodder is present and accounted for."

"But most of the livestock was eaten at, like the heifer," Parker objected.

"By definition, nuts have abnormal tastes," the sergeant replied "Or the eating might have been done later, by foxes."

"I hope so; that'd let me out," Parker said.

"Ha, listen to the man!" the private howled, stopping the car at the end of the lane. "He thinks a nut with a machete and a Tarzan complex is just good clean fun. Which way, now?"

"Well, let's see." The sergeant had unfolded a quadrangle sheet; the game protector leanded forward to look at it over his shoulder. The sergeant ran a finger from one to another of a series of variously colored crosses which had been marked on the map.

"Monday night, over here on Copperhead Mountain, that cow was killed," he said. "The next night, about ten o'clock, that sheep-flock was hit, on this side of Copperhead, right about here. Early Wednesday night, that mule got slashed up in the woods back of the Weston farm. It was only slightly injured; must have kicked the whatzit and got away, but the whatzit wasn't too badly hurt, because a few hours later, it hit that turkey-flock on the Rhymer farm. And last night, it did that." He jerked a thumb over his shoulder at the Strawmyer farm. "See, following the ridges, working toward the southeast, avoiding open ground, killing only at night. Could be a bobcat, at that."

"Or Jink's maniac with the machete," Parker agreed. "Let's go up by Hindman's gap and see if we can see anything."

They turned, after a while, into a rutted dirt road, which deteriorated steadily into a grass-grown track through the woods. Finally, they stopped, and the private backed off the road. The three men got out; Parker with his Winchester, the sergeant checking the drum of a Thompson, and the private pumping a buckshot shell into the chamber of a riot gun. For half an hour, they followed the brush-grown trail beside the little stream; once, they passed a dark gray commercial-model jeep, backed to one side. Then they came to the head of the gap.

A man wearing a tweed coat, tan field boots, and khaki breeches, was sitting on a log, smoking a pipe; he had a bolt-action rifle across his knees, and a pair of binoculars hung from his neck. He seemed about thirty years old, and any bobby-soxer's idol of the screen would have envied him the handsome regularity of his strangely immobile features. As Parker and the two State policemen approached, he rose, slinging his rifle, and greeted them.

"Sergeant Haines, isn't it?" he asked pleasantly. "Are you gentlemen out hunting the critter, too?"

"Good afternoon, Mr. Lee. I thought that was your jeep I saw, down the road a little." The sergeant turned to the others. "Mr. Richard Lee; staying at the old Kinchwalter place, the other side of Rutter's Fort. This is Mr. Parker, the district game protector. And Private Zinkowski." He glanced at the rifle. "Are you out hunting for it, too?"

"Yes, I thought I might find something, up here. What do you think it is?"

"I don't know," the sergeant admitted. "It could be a bobcat. Canada lynx. Jinx, here, has a theory that it's some escapee from the paper-doll factory, with a machete. Me, I hope not, but I'm not ignoring the possibility."

The man with the matinee-idol's face nodded. "It could be a lynx. I understand they're not unknown, in this section."

"We paid bounties on two in this county, in the last year," Parker said. "Odd rifle you have there; mind if I look at it?"

"Not at all." The man who had been introduced as Richard Lee unslung and handed it over. "The chamber's loaded," he cautioned.

"I never saw one like this," Parker said. "Foreign?"

"I think so. I don't know anything about it; it belongs to a friend of mine, who loaned it to me. I think the action's German, or Czech; the rest of it's a custom job, by some West Coast gunmaker. It's chambered for some ultra-velocity wildcat load."

The rifle passed from hand to hand; the three men examined it in turn, commenting admiringly.

"You find anything, Mr. Lee?" the sergeant asked, handing it back.

"Not a trace." The man called Lee slung the rifle and began to dump the ashes from his pipe. "I was along the top of this ridge for about a mile on either side of the gap, and down the other side as far as Hindman's Run; I didn't find any tracks, or any indication of where it had made a kill."

The game protector nodded, turning to Sergeant Haines.

"There's no use us going any farther," he said. "Ten to one, it followed that line of woods back of Strawmyer's, and crossed over to the other ridge. I think our best best would be the hollow at the head of Lowrie's Run. What do you think?"

The sergeant agreed. The man called Richard Lee began

to refill his pipe methodically.

"I think I shall stay here for a while, but I believe you're right. Lowrie's Run, or across Lowrie's Gap into Coon Valley," he said.

After Parker and the State policemen had gone, the man whom they had addressed as Richard Lee returned to his log and sat smoking, his rifle across his knees. From time to time, he glanced at his wrist watch and raised his head to listen. At length, faint in the distance, he heard the sound of a motor starting.

Instantly, he was on his feet. From the end of the hollow log on which he had been sitting, he produced a canvas musette-bag. Walking briskly to a patch of damp ground beside the little stream, he leaned the rifle against a tree and opened the bag. First, he took out a pair of gloves of some greenish, rubberlike substance, and put them on, drawing the long gauntlets up over his coat sleeves. Then he produced a bottle and unscrewed the cap. Being careful to avoid splashing his clothes, he went about, pouring a clear liquid upon the ground in several places. Where he poured, white vapors rose, and twigs and grass grumbled into brownish dust. After he had replaced the cap and returned the bottle to the bag, he waited for a few minutes, then took a spatula from the musette and dug where he had poured the fluid, prying loose four black, irregular-shaped lumps of matter, which he carried to the running water and washed carefully, before wrapping them and putting them in the bag, along with the gloves. Then he slung bag and rifle and started down the trail to where he had parked the jeep.

Half an hour later, after driving through the little farming village of Rutter's Fort, he pulled into the barnyard of a rundown farm and backed through the open doors of the barn.

He closed the double doors behind him, and barred them from within. Then he went to the rear wall of the barn, which was much closer to the front than the outside dimensions of the barn would have indicated.

He took from his pocket a black object like an automatic pencil. Hunting over the rough plank wall, he found a small hole and inserted the pointed end of the pseudo-pencil, pressing on the other end. For an instant, nothing happened. Then a ten-foot-square section of the wall receded two feet and slid noiselessly to one side. The section which had slid inward had been built of three-inch steel, masked by a thin covering of boards; the wall around it was two-foot concrete, similarly camouflaged. He stepped quickly inside.

Fumbling at the right side of the opening, he found a switch and flicked it. Instantly, the massive steel plate slid back into place with a soft, oily click. As it did, lights came on within the hidden room, disclosing a great semiglobe of some fine metallic mesh, thirty feet in diameter and fifteen in height. There was a sliding door at one side of this; the man called Richard Lee opened and entered through it, closing it behind him. Then he turned to the center of the hollow dome, where an armchair was placed in front of a small desk below a large instrument panel. The gauges and dials on the panel, and the levers and switches and buttons on the desk control board, were all lettered and numbered with characters not of the Roman alphabet or the Arabic notation, and, within instant reach of the occupant of the chair, a pistol-like weapon lay on the desk. It had a conventional index-finger trigger and a hand-fit grip, but, instead of a tubular barrel, two slender parallel metal rods extended about four inches forward of the receiver, joined together at what would correspond to the muzzle by a streamlined knob of some light blue ceramic or plastic substance.

The man with the handsome immobile face deposited his rifle and musette on the floor beside the chair and sat down. First, he picked up the pistol-like weapon and checked it, and then he examined the many instruments on the panel in front of him. Finally, he flicked a switch on the control board.

At once, a small humming began, from some point overhead. It wavered and shrilled and mounted in intensity, and then fell to a steady monotone. The dome about him flickered with a queer, cold iridescence, and slowly vanished. The hidden room vanished, and he was looking into the shadowy interior of a deserted barn. The barn vanished; blue sky appeared above, streaked with wisps of high cirrus cloud. The autumn landscape flickered unreally. Buildings appeared and vanished, and other buildings came and went in a twinkling. All around him, half-seen shapes moved briefly and disappeared.

Once, the figure of a man appeared, inside the circle of the dome. He had an angry, brutal face, and he wore a black tunic piped with silver, and black breeches, and polished black boots, and there was an insignia, composed of a cross and thunderbolt, on his cap. He held an automatic pistol in his hand.

Instantly, the man at the desk snatched up his own weapon and thumbed off the safety, but before he could lift and aim it, the intruder stumbled and passed outside the force-field which surrounded the chair and instruments.

For a while, there were fires raging outside, and for a while, the man at the desk was surrounded by a great hall, with a high, vaulted ceiling, through which figures flitted and

vanished. For a while, there were vistas of deep forests, always set in the same background of mountains and always under the same blue cirrus-laced sky. There was an interval of flickering blue-white light, of unbearable intensity. Then the man at the desk was surrounded by the interior of vast industrial works. The moving figures around him slowed, and became more distinct. For an instant, the man in the chair grinned as he found himself looking into a big washroom, where a tall blond girl was taking a shower bath, and a pert little redhead was vigorously drying herself with a towel. The dome grew visible, coruscating with many-colored lights and then the humming died and the dome became a cold and inert mesh of fine white metal. A green light above flashed on and off slowly.

He stabbed a button and flipped a switch, then got to his feet, picking up his rifle and musette and fumbling under his shirt for a small mesh bag, from which he took an inch-wide disk of blue plastic. Unlocking a container on the instrument panel, he removed a small roll of solidograph-film, which he stowed in his bag. Then he slid open the door and emerged into his own dimension of space-time.

Outside was a wide hallway, with a pale green floor, paler green walls, and a ceiling of greenish off-white. A big hole had been cut to accommodate the dome, and across the hallway a desk had been set up, and at it sat a clerk in a pale blue tunic, who was just taking the audio-plugs of a music-box out of his ears. A couple of policemen in green uniforms, with ultrasonic paralyzers dangling by thongs from their left wrists and holstered sigma-ray needlers like the one on the desk inside the dome, were kidding with some girls in vivid orange and scarlet and green smocks. One of these, in bright green, was a duplicate of the one he had seen rubbing herself down with a towel.

"Here comes your boss-man," one of the girls told the cops, as he approached. They both turned and saluted casually. The man who had lately been using the name of Richard Lee responded to their greeting and went to the desk. The policemen grasped their paralyzers, drew their needlers, and hurried into the dome.

Taking the disk of blue plastic from his packet, he handed it to the clerk at the desk, who dropped it into a slot in the voder in front of him. Instantly, a mechanical voice responded:

"Verkan Vall, blue-seal noble, hereditary Mavrad of Nerros. Special Chief's Assistant, Paratime Police, special assignment. Subject to no orders below those of Tortha Karf,

Chief of Paratime Police. To be given all courtesies and co-operation within the Paratime Transposition Code and the Police Powers Code. Further particulars?"

The clerk pressed the "no"-button. The blue sigil fell out the release-slot and was handed back to its bearer, who was drawing up his left sleeve.

"You'll want to be sure I'm *your* Verkan Vall, I suppose?" he said, extending his arm.

"Yes, quite, sir."

The clerk touched his arm with a small instrument which swabbed it with antiseptic, drew a minute blood-sample, and medicated the needle prick, all in one almost painless operation. He put the blood-drop on a slide and inserted it at one side of a comparison microscope, nodding. It showed the same distinctive permanent colloid pattern as the sample he had ready for comparison; the colloid pattern given in infancy by injection to the man in front of him, to set him apart from all the myriad other Verkan Valls on every other probability-line of paratime.

"Right, sir," the clerk nodded.

The two policemen came out of the dome, their needlers holstered and their vigilance relaxed. They were lighting cigarettes as they emerged.

"It's all right, sir," one of them said. "You didn't bring anything in with you, this trip."

The other cop chuckled. "Remember that Fifth Level wild-man who came in on the freight conveyor at Jandar, last month?" he asked.

If he was hoping that some of the girls would want to know what wild-man, it was a vain hope. With a blue-seal mavrad around, what chance did a couple of ordinary coppers have? The girls were already converging on Verkan Vall.

"When are you going to get that monstrosity out of our rest room," the little redhead in green coveralls was demanding. "If it wasn't for that thing, I'd be taking a shower, right now."

"You were just finishing one, about fifty paraseconds off, when I came through," Verkan Vall told her.

The girl looked at him in obviously feigned indignation. "Why, you— You *parapeeper!*"

Verkan Vall chuckled and turned to the clerk. "I want a strato-rocket and pilot, for Dhergabar, right away. Call Dhergabar Paratime Police Field and give them my ETA; have an air-taxi meet me, and have the chief notified that I'm coming in. Extraordinary report. Keep a guard over the conveyor; I think I'm going to need it, again, soon." He turned to the little redhead. "Want to show me the way out of here, to the rocket field?" he asked.

Outside, on the open landing field, Verkan Vall glanced up at the sky, then looked at his watch. It had been twenty minutes since he had backed the jeep into the barn on that distant other time-line; the same delicate lines of white cirrus were etched across the blue above. The constancy of the weather, even across two hundred thousand parayears of perpendicular time, never failed to impress him. The long curve of the mountains was the same, and they were mottled with the same autumn colors, but where the little village of Rutter's Fort stood on that other line of probability, the white towers of an apartment-city rose—the living quarters of the plant personnel.

The rocket that was to take him to headquarters was being hoisted with a crane and lowered into the firing-stand, and he walked briskly toward it, his rifle and musette slung. A boyish-looking pilot was on the platform, opening the door of the rocket; he stood aside for Verkan Vall to enter, then followed and closed it, dogging it shut while his passenger stowed his bag and rifle and strapped himself into a seat.

"Dhergabar Commercial Terminal, sir?" the pilot asked, taking the adjoining seat at the controls.

"Paratime Police Field, back of the Paratime Administration Building."

"Right, sir. Twenty seconds to blast, when you're ready."

"Ready now." Verkan Vall relaxed, counting seconds subconsciously.

The rocket trembled, and Verkan Vall felt himself being pushed gently back against the upholstery. The seats, and the pilot's instrument panel in front of them, swung on gimbals, and the finger of the indicator swept slowly over a ninety-degree arc as the rocket rose and leveled. By then, the high cirrus clouds Verkan Vall had watched from the field were far below; they were well into the stratosphere.

There would be nothing to do, now, for the three hours in which the rocket sped northward across the pole and southward to Dhergabar; the navigation was entirely in the electronic hands of the robot controls. Verkan Vall got out his pipe and lit it; the pilot lit a cigarette.

"That's an odd pipe, sir," the pilot said. "Out-time item?"

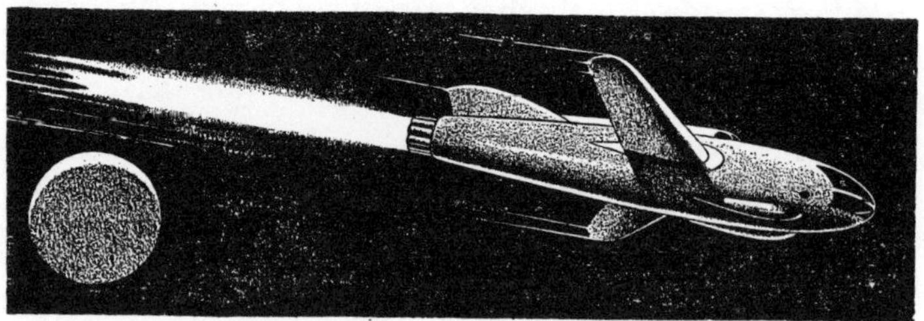

"Yes, Fourth Probability Level; typical of the whole paratime belt I was working in." Verkan Vall handed it over for inspection. "The bowl's natural brier-root; the stem's a sort of plastic made from the sap of certain tropical trees. The little white dot is the maker's trademark; it's made of elephant tusk."

"Sounds pretty crude to me, sir." The pilot handed it back. "Nice workmanship, though. Looks like good machine production."

"Yes. The sector I was on is really quite advanced, for an electro-chemical civilization. That weapon I brought back with me—that solid-missile projector—is typical of most Fourth Level culture. Moving parts machined to the closest tolerances, and interchangeable with similar parts of all similar weapons. The missile is a small bolt of cupro-alloy coated lead, propelled by expanding gases from the ignition of some nitro-cellulose compound. Most of their scientific advance occurred within the past century, and most of that in the past forty years. Of course, the life-expectancy on that level is only about seventy years."

"Humph! I'm seventy-eight, last birthday," the boyish-looking pilot snorted. "Their medical science must be mostly witchcraft!"

"Until quite recently, it was," Verkan Vall agreed. "Same story there as in everything else—rapid advancement in the past few decades, after thousands of years of cultural inertia."

"You know, sir, I don't really understand this paratime stuff," the pilot confessed. "I know that all time is totally present, and that every moment has its own past-future line of event-sequence, and that all events in space-time occur according to maximum probability, but I just don't get this alternate probability stuff, at all. If something exists, it's because it's the maximum-probability effect of prior causes; why does anything else exist on any other time-line?"

Verkan Vall blew smoke at the air-renovator. A lecture on paratime theory would nicely fill in the three-hour interval until the landing at Dhergabar. At least, this kid was asking intelligent questions.

"Well, you know the principle of time-passage, I suppose?" he began.

"Yes, of course; Rhogom's Doctrine. The basis of most of our psychical science. We exist perpetually at all moments within our life-span; our extraphysical ego component passes from the ego existing at one moment to the ego existing at the next. During unconsciousness, the EPC is 'time-free'; it may detach, and connect at some other moment, with the ego existing at that time-point. That's how we precog. We take an autohypno and recover memories brought back from the future moment and buried in the subconscious mind."

"That's right," Verkan Vall told him. "And even without the autohypno, a lot of precognitive matter leaks out of the subconscious and into the conscious mind, usually in distorted forms, or else inspires 'instinctive' acts, the motivation for which is not brought to the level of consciousness. For instance, suppose, you're walking along North Promenade, in Dhergabar, and you come to the Martian Palace Cafe, and you go in for a drink, and meet some girl, and strike up an acquaintance with her. This chance acquaintance develops into a love affair, and a year later, out of jealousy, she rays you half a dozen times with a needler."

"Just about that happened to a friend of mine, not long ago," the pilot said. "Go on, sir."

"Well, in the microsecond or so before you die—or afterward, for that matter, because we know that the extraphysical component survives physical destruction—your EPC slips back a couple of years and re-connects at some point pastward of your first meeting with this girl, and carries with it memories of everything up to the moment of detachment, all of which are indelibly recorded in your subconscious mind. So, when you re-experience the event of standing outside the Martian Palace with a thirst, you go on to the Starway, or Nhergal's, or some other bar. In both cases, on both time-lines, you follow the line of maximum probability; in the second case, your subconscious future memories are an added causal factor."

"And when I back-slip, after I've been needled, I generate a new time-line? Is that it?"

Verkan Vall made a small sound of impatience. "No such thing!" he exclaimed. "It's semantically inadmissible to talk about the total presence of time with one breath and about generating new time-lines with the next. *All* time-lines are totally present, in perpetual co-existence. The theory is that the EPC passes from one moment, on one time-line, to the next moment on the next line, so that the true passage of the EPC from moment to moment is a two-dimensional diagonal. So, in the case we're using, the event of your going into the Martian Palace exists on one time-line, and the event of your passing along to the Starway exists on another, but both are events in real existence.

"Now, what we do, in paratime transposition, is to build up a hypertemporal field to include the time-line we want to reach, and then shift over to it. Same point in the plenum; same point in primary time—plus primary time elapsed during mechanical and electronic lag in the relays—but a different line of secondary time."

"Then why don't we have past-future time travel on our own time-line?" the pilot wanted to know.

That was a question every paratimer has to answer, every time he talks paratime to the laity. Verkan Vall had been expecting it; he answered patiently.

"The Ghaldron-Hesthor field-generator is like every other mechanism; it can operate in the area of primary time in which it exists. It can transpose to any other time-line, and carry with it anything inside its field, but it can't go outside its own temporal area of existence, any more than a bullet from that rifle can hit the target a week before it's fired," Verkan Vall pointed out. "Anything inside the field is supposed to be unaffected by anything outside. *Supposed to be* is the way to put it; it doesn't always work. Once in a while, something pretty nasty gets picked up in transit." He thought, briefly, of the man in the black tunic. "That's why we have armed guards at terminals."

"Suppose you pick up a blast from a nucleonic bomb," the pilot asked, "or something red-hot, or radioactive?"

"We have a monument, at Paratime Police Headquarters, in Dhergabar, bearing the names of our own personnel who didn't make it back. It's a large monument; over the past ten thousand years, it's been inscribed with quite a few names."

"You can have it; I'll stick to rockets!" the pilot replied. "Tell me another thing, though: What's all this about levels, and sectors, and belts? What's the difference?"

"Purely arbitrary terms. There are five main probability levels, derived from the five possible outcomes of the attempt to colonize this planet, seventy-five thousand years ago. We're on the First Level—complete success, and colony fully established. The Fifth Level is the probabilty of complete failure—no human population established on this planet, and indigenous quasi-human life evolved indigenously. On the Fourth Level, the colonists evidently met with some disaster and lost all memory of their extraterrestrial origin, as well as all extraterrestrial culture. As far as they know, they are an indigenous race; they have a long pre-history of stone-age savagery.

"Sectors are areas of paratime on any level in which the prevalent culture has a common origin and common characteristics. They are divided more or less arbitrarily into sub-sectors. Belts are areas within sub-sectors where conditions are the result of recent alternate probabilities. For instance, I've just come from the Europo-American Sector of the Fourth Level, an area of about ten thousand parayears in depth, in which the dominant civilization developed on the North-West Continent of the Major Land Mass, and spread from there to the Minor Land Mass. The line on which I was operating is also part of a sub-sector of about three thousand parayears' depth, and a belt developing from one of several probable outcomes of a war concluded about three elapsed years ago. On that time-line, the field at the Hagraban Synthetics Works, where we took off, is part of an abandoned farm; on the site of Hagraban City is a little farming village. Those things are there, right now, both in primary time and in the plenum. They are about two hundred and fifty thousand parayears perpendicular to each other, and each is of the same general order of reality."

The red light overhead flashed on. The pilot looked into his visor and put his hands to the manual controls, in case of failure of the robot controls. The rocket landed smoothly, however; there was a slight jar as it was grappled by the crane and hoisted upright, the seats turning in their gimbals. Pilot and passenger unstrapped themselves and hurried through the refrigerated outlet and away from the glowing-hot rocket.

An air-taxi, emblazoned with the device of the Paratime Police, was waiting. Verkan Vall said goodby to the rocket-pilot and took his seat beside the pilot of the aircab; the latter lifted his vehicle above the building level and then set it down on the landing-stage of the Paratime Police Building in a long, side-swooping glide. An express elevator took Verkan Vall down to one of the middle stages, where he showed his sigil to the guard outside the door of Tortha Karf's office and was admitted at once.

The Paratime Police chief rose from behind his semicircular desk, with its array of keyboards and viewing-screens and communicators. He was a big man, well past his two hundredth year; his hair was iron-gray and thinning in front, he had begun to grow thick at the waist, and his calm features bore the lines of middle age. He wore the dark-green uniform of the Paratime Police.

"Well, Vall," he greeted. "Everything secure?"

"Not exactly, sir." Verkan Vall came around the desk, deposited his rifle and bag on the floor, and sat down in one of the spare chairs. "I'll have to go back again."

"So?" His chief lit a cigarette and waited.

"I traced Gavran Sarn." Verkan Vall got out his pipe and began to fill it. "But that's only the beginning. I have to trace something else. Gavran Sarn exceeded his Paratime permit, and took one of his pets along. A Venusian nighthound."

Tortha Karf's expression did not alter; it merely grew more intense. He used one of the short, semantically ugly terms which serve, in place of profanity, as the emotional release of a race that has forgotten all the taboos and terminologies of supernaturalistic religion and sex inhibition.

"You're sure of this, of course." It was less a question than a statement.

Verkan Vall bent and took cloth-wrapped objects from his bag, unwrapping them and laying them on the desk. They were casts, in hard black plastic, of the footprints of some large three-toed animal.

"What do these look like, sir?" he asked.

Tortha Karf fingered them and nodded. Then he became as visibly angry as a man of his ciilization and culture-level ever permitted himself.

"What does that fool think we have a Paratime Code for?" he demanded. "It's entirely illegal to transpose any extraterrestrial animal or object to any time-line on which space-travel is unknown. I don't care if he is a green-seal thavrad; he'll face charges, when he gets back, for this!"

"He *was* a green-seal thavrad," Verkan Vall corrected. "And he won't be coming back."

"I hope you didn't have to deal summarily with him," Tortha Karf said. "With his title, and social position, and his family's political importance, that might make difficulties. Not that it wouldn't be all right with me, of course, but we never seem to be able to make either the Management or the public realize the extremities to which we are forced, at times." He sighed. "We probably never shall."

Verkan Vall smiled faintly. "Oh, no, sir; nothing like that. He was dead before I transposed to that time-line. He was killed when he wrecked a self-propelled vehicle he was using. One of those Fourth Level automobiles. I posed as a relative and tried to claim his body for the burial-ceremony observed on that cultural level, but was told that it had been completely destroyed by fire when the fuel tank of this automobile burned. I was given certain of his effects which had passed through the fire; I found his sigil concealed inside what appeared to be a cigarette case." He took a green disk from the bag and laid it on the desk. "There's no question; Gavran Sarn died in the wreck of that automobile."

"And the nighthound?"

"It was in the car with him, but it escaped. You know how fast those things are. I found that track"—he indicated one of the black casts—"in some dried mud near the scene of the wreck. As you see, the cast is slightly defective. The others were fresh this morning, when I made them."

"And what have you done so far?"

"I rented an old farm near the scene of the wreck, and installed my field-generator there. It runs through to the Hagraban Synthetics Works, about a hundred miles east of Thalna-Jarvizar. I have my this-line terminal in the girls' rest room at the durable plastics factory; handled that on a local police-power writ. Since then, I've been hunting for the nighthound. I think I can find it, but I'll need some special equipment, and a hypno-mech indoctrination. That's why I came back."

• • •

"Has it been attracting any attention?" Tortha Karf asked anxiously.

"Killing cattle in the locality; causing considerable excitement. Fortunately, it's a locality of forested mountains and valley farms, rather than a built-up industrial district. Local police and wild game protection officers are concerned; all the farmers excited and going armed. The theory is that it's either a wildcat of some sort, or a maniac armed with a cutlass. Either theory would conform, more or less, to the nature of its depredations. Nobody has actually seen it."

"That's good!" Tortha Karf was relieved. "Well, you'll have to go and bring it out, or kill it and obliterate the body. You know why, as well as I do."

"Certainly, sir," Verkan Vall replied. "In a primitive culture, things like this would be assigned supernatural explanations, and imbedded in the locally accepted religion. But this culture, while nominally religious, is highly rationalistic in practice. Typical lag-effect, characteristic of all expanding cultures. And this Europo-American Sector really has an expanding culture. A hundred and fifty years ago, the inhabitants of this particular time-line didn't even know how to apply steam power; now they've begun to release nuclear energy, in a few crude forms."

Tortha Karf whistled, softly. "That's quite a jump. There's a sector that'll be in for trouble in the next few centuries."

"That is realized, locally, sir." Verkan Vall concentrated on relighting his pipe, for a moment, then continued: "I would predict space-travel on that sector within the next century. Maybe the next half-century, at least to the Moon. And the art of taxidermy is very highly developed. Now, suppose some farmer shoots that thing; what would he do with it, sir?"

Tortha Karf grunted. "Nice logic, Vall. On a most uncomfortable possibility. He'd have it mounted, and it'd be put in a museum, somewhere. And as soon as the first spaceship reaches Venus, and they find those things in a wild state, they'll have the mounted specimen identified."

"Exactly. And then, instead of beating their brains about *where* their specimen came from, they'll begin asking *when* it came from. They're quite capable of such reasoning, even now."

"A hundred years isn't a particularly long time," Tortha Karf considered. "I'll be retired, then, but you'll have my job, and it'll be your headache. You'd better get this cleaned up, now, while it can be handled. What are you going to do?"

"I'm not sure, now, sir. I want a hypno-mech indoctrination, first." Verkan Vall gestured toward the communicator on the desk. "May I?" he asked.

"Certainly." Tortha Karf slid the instrument across the desk. "Anything you want."

"Thank you, sir." Verkan Vall snapped on the code-index, found the symbol he wanted, and then punched it on the keyboard. "Special Chief's Assistant Verkan Vall," he identified himself. "Speaking from office of Tortha Karf, Chief Paratime Police. I want a complete hypno-mech on Venusian nighthounds, emphasis on wild state, special emphasis domesticated nighthounds reverted to wild state in terrestrial surroundings, extra-special emphasis hunting techniques applicable to same. The word 'nighthound' will do for trigger-symbol." He turned to Tortha Karf. "Can I take it here?"

Tortha Karf nodded, pointing to a row of booths along the far wall of the office.

"Make set-up for wired transmission; I'll take it here."

"Very well, sir; in fifteen minutes," a voice replied out of the communicator.

Verkan Vall slid the communicator back. "By the way, sir; I had a hitchhiker, on the way back. Carried him about a hundred or so parayears; picked him up about three hundred parayears after leaving my other-line terminal. Nasty-looking fellow, in a black uniform; looked like one of those private army storm troopers you find all through that sector. Armed, and hostile. I thought I'd have to ray him, but he blundered outside the field almost at once. I have a record, if you'd care to see it."

"Yes, put it on." Tortha Karf gestured toward the solidograph-projector. "It's set for miniature reproduction here on the desk; that be all right?"

Verkan Vall nodded, getting out the film and loading it into the projector. When he pressed a button, a dome of radiance appeared on the desk top, two feet in width and a foot in height. In the middle of this appeared a small solidograph-image of the interior of the conveyor, showing the desk, and the control board, and the figure of Verkan Vall seated at it. The little figure of the storm trooper appeared, pistol in hand. The little Verkan Vall snatched up his tiny needler; the storm trooper moved into one side of the dome and vanished.

Verkan Vall flipped a switch and cut out the image.

"Yes. I don't know what causes that, but it happens, now and then," Tortha Karf said. "Usually at the beginning of a transposition. I remember, when I was just a kid, about a hundred and fifty years ago—a hundred and thirty-nine, to be exact—I picked up a fellow on the Fourth Level, just about where you're operating, and dragged him a couple of hundred parayears. I went back to find him and return him to his own time-line, but before I could locate him, he'd been arrested by the local authorities as a suspicious character, and got himself shot trying to escape. I felt badly about that, but—" Tortha Karf shrugged. "Anything else happen on the trip?"

"I ran through a belt of intermittent nucleonic bombing on the Second Level." Verkan Vall mentioned an approximate paratime location.

"Aaagh! That Khiftan civilization—by courtesy so called!" Tortha Karf pulled a wry face. "I suppose the intra-family enmities of the Hvadka Dynasty have reached critical mass again. They'll fool around till they blast themselves back to the stone age."

"Intellectually, they're about there, now. I had to operate in that sector once— Oh, yes, another thing, sir. This rifle." Verkan Vall picked it up, emptied the magazine and handed it to his superior. "The supplies office slipped up on this; it's not appropriate to my line of operation. It's a lovely rifle, but it's about two hundred percent in advance of existing arms design on my line. It excited the curiosity of a couple of police officers and a game-protector, who should be familiar with the weapons of their own time-line. I evaded by disclaiming ownership or intimate knowledge, and they seemed satisfied, but it worried me."

"Yes. That was made in our duplicating shops here in Dhergabar." Tortha Karf carried it to a photographic bench, behind his desk. "I'll have it checked, while you're taking your hypno-mech. Want to exchange it for something authentic?"

"Why, no, sir. It's been identified to me, and I'd excite less suspicion with it than I would if I abandoned it and mysteriously acquired another rifle. I just wanted a check, and Supplies warned to be more careful in future."

Tortha Karf nodded approvingly. The young Mavrad of Nerros was thinking as a paratimer should.

"What's the designation of your line again?"

Verkan Vall told him. It was a short numerical term of six places, but it expressed a number of the order of ten to the fortieth power, exact to the last digit. Tortha Karf repeated it into his stenomemograph, with explanatory comment.

"There seems to be quite a few things going wrong, in that area," he said. "Let's see now."

He punched the designation on a keyboard; instantly, it appeared on a translucent screen in front of him. He punched another combination, and, at the top of the screen under the number, there appeared: EVENTS, PAST ELAPSED FIVE YEARS.

He punched again; below this line appeared the sub-heading: EVENTS INVOLVING PARATIME TRANSPOSITION.

Another code-combination added a third line: (ATTRACTING PUBLIC NOTICE AMONG INHABITANTS.)

He pressed the "start" button; the headings vanished, to be replaced by page after page of print, succeeding one another on the screen as the two men read. They told strange and apparently disconnected stories—of unexplained fires and explosions; of people vanishing without trace; of unaccountable disasters to aircraft. There were many stories of an epidemic of mysterious disk-shaped objects seen in the sky, singly or in numbers. To each account was appended one or more reference-numbers. Sometimes Tortha Karf or Verkan Vall would punch one of these, and read, on an adjoining screen, the explanatory matter referred to.

Finally Tortha Karf leaned back and lit a fresh cigarette.

"Yes, indeed, Vall; very definitely we will have to take action in the matter of the runaway nighthound of the late Gavran Sarn," he said. "I'd forgotten that that was the time-line onto which the *Andrath* expedition launched those anti-grav disks. If this extraterrestrial monstrosity turns up, on the heels of that 'Flying Saucer' business, everybody above the order of intelligence of a cretin will suspect some connection."

"What really happened, in the *Ardrath* matter?" Verkan

Vall inquired. "I was on the Third Level, on that Luvarian Empire operation, at the time."

"That's right; you missed that. Well, it was one of these joint operation things. The Paratime Commission and the Space Patrol were experimenting with a new technique for throwing a spaceship into paratime. They used the cruiser *Ardrath*, Kalzarn Jann commanding. Went into space about halfway to the Moon and took up orbit, keeping on the sunlit side of the planet to avoid being observed. That was all right. But then, Captain Kalzarn ordered away a flight of antigrav disks, fully manned, to take pictures, and finally authorized a landing in the western mountain range, Northern Continent, Minor Land-Mass. That's when the trouble started."

He flipped the run-back switch, till he had recovered the page he wanted. Verkan Vall read of a Fourth Level aviator, in his little airscrew-drive craft, sighting nine high-flying saucerlike objects.

"That was how it began," Tortha Karf told him. "Before long, as other incidents of the same sort occurred, our people on that line began sending back to know what was going on. Naturally, from the different descriptions of these 'saucers', they recognized the objects as antigrav landing-disks from a spaceship. So I went to the Commission and raised atomic blazes about it, and the *Ardrath* was ordered to confine operations to the lower areas of the Fifth Level. Then our people on that time-line went to work with corrective action. Here."

He wiped the screen and then began punching combinations. Page after page appeared, bearing accounts of people who had claimed to have seen the mysterious disks, and each report was more fantastic than the last.

"The standard smother-out technique," Verkan Vall

grinned. "I only heard a little talk about the 'Flying Saucers', and all of that was in joke. In that order of culture, you can always discredit one true story by setting up ten others, palpably false, parallel to it— Wasn't that the time-line the Tharmax Trading Corporation almost lost their paratime license on?"

"That's right; it was! They bought up all the cigarettes, and caused a conspicuous shortage, after Fourth Level cigarettes had been introduced on this line and had become popular. They should have spread their purchases over a number of lines, and kept them within the local supply-demand frame. And they also got into trouble with the local government for selling unrationed petrol and automobile tires. We had to send in a special-operations group, and they came closer to having to engage in out-time local politics than I care to think of." Tortha Karf quoted a line from a currently popular song about the sorrows of a policeman's life. "We're jugglers, Vall; trying to keep our traders and sociological observers and tourists and plain idiots like the late Gavran Sarn out of trouble; trying to prevent panics and disturbances and dislocations of local economy as a result of our operations; trying to keep out of out-time politics—and, at all times, at all costs and hazards, by all means, guarding the secret of paratime transposition. Sometimes I wish Ghaldron Karf and Hesthor Ghrom had strangled in their cradles!"

Verkan Vall shook his head. "No, chief," he said. "You don't mean that; not really," he said. "We've been paratiming for the past ten thousand years. When the Ghaldron-Hesthor trans-temporal field was discovered, our ancestors had pretty well exhausted the resources of this planet. We had a world population of half a billion, and it was all they could do to keep alive. After we began paratime transposition, our population climbed to ten billion, and there it stayed for the last eight thousand years. Just enough of us to enjoy our planet and the other planets of the system to the fullest; enough of everything for everybody that nobody needs fight anybody for anything. We've tapped the resources of those other worlds on other time-lines, a little here, a little there, and not enough to really hurt anybody. We've left our mark in a few places—the Dakota Badlands, and the Gobi, on the Fourth Level, for instance—but we've done no great damage to any of them."

"Except the time they blew up half the Southern Island Continent, over about five hundred parayears on the Third Level," Tortha Karf mentioned.

"Regrettable accident, to be sure," Verkan Vall conceded. "And look how much we've learned from the experiences of those other time-lines. During the Crisis, after the Fourth Interplanetary War, we might have adopted Palnar Sarn's 'Dictatorship of the Chosen' scheme, if we hadn't seen what an exactly similar scheme had done to the Jak-Hakka Civilization, on the Second Level. When Palnar Sarn was told about that, he went into paratime to see for himself, and when he returned, he renounced his proposal in horror."

Tortha Karf nodded. He wouldn't be making any mistake in turning his post over to the Mavrad of Nerros on his retirement.

"Yes, Vall; I know," he said. "But when you've been at this desk as long as I have, you'll have a sour moment or two, now and then, too."

A blue light flashed over one of the booths across the room. Verkan Vall got to his feet, removing his coat and hanging it on the back of his chair, and crossed the room rolling up his left shirt sleeve. There was a relaxer-chair in the booth, with a blue plastic helmet above it. He glanced at the indicator screen to make sure he was getting the indoctrination he called for, and then sat down in the chair and lowered the helmet over his head, inserting the ear plugs and fastening the chin strap. Then he touched his left arm with an injector which was lying on the arm of the chair, and at the same time flipped the starter switch.

Soft, slow music began to chant out of the earphones. The insidious fingers of the drug blocked off his senses, one by one. The music diminished, and the words of the hypnotic formula lulled him to sleep.

He woke, hearing the lively strains of dance music. For a while, he lay relaxed. Then he snapped off the switch, took out the ear plugs, removed the helmet and rose to his feet. Deep in his subconscious mind was the entire body of knowledge about the Venusian nighthound. He mentally pronounced the word, and at once it began flooding into his conscious mind. He knew the animal's evolutionary history, its anatomy, its characteristics, its dietary and reproductive habits, how it hunted, how it fought its enemies, how it eluded pursuit, and how best it could be tracked down and killed. He nodded. Already, a plan for dealing with Gavran Sarn's renegade pet was taking shape in his mind.

• • •

He picked a plastic cup from the dispensor, filled it from a cooler-tap with amber-colored spiced wine, and drank, tossing the cup into the disposal-bin. He placed a fresh injector on the arm of the chair, ready for the next user of the booth. Then he emerged, glancing at his Fourth Level wrist watch and

mentally translating to the First Level time-scale. Three hours had passed; there had been more to learn about his quarry than he had expected.

Tortha Karf was sitting behind his desk, smoking a cigarette. It seemed as though he had not moved since Verkan Vall had left him, though the special agent knew that he had dined, attended several conferences, and done many other things.

"I checked up on your hitchhiker, Vall," the chief said. "We won't bother about him. He's a member of something called the Christian Avengers—one of those typical Europo-American race-and-religious hate groups. He belongs in a belt that is the outcome of the Hitler victory of 1940, whatever that was. Something unpleasant, I dare say. We don't owe him anything; people of that sort should be stepped on like cockroaches. And he won't make any more trouble on the line where you dropped him than they have there already. It's in a belt of complete social and political anarchy; somebody probably shot him as soon as he emerged, because he wasn't wearing the right sort of a uniform. Nineteen-forty what, by the way?"

"Elapsed years since the birth of some religious leader," Verkan Vall explained. "And did you find out about my rifle?"

"Oh, yes. It's a reproduction of something that's called a Sharp's Model '37,235 Ultraspeed-Express. Made on an adjoining paratime belt by a company that went out of business sixty-seven years ago, elapsed time, on your line of operation. What made the difference was the Second War Between The States. I don't know what that was, either—I'm not too well up on Fourth Level history—but whatever, your line of operation didn't have it. Probably just as well for them, though they very likely had something else, as bad or worse. I put in a complaint to Supplies about it, and got you some more ammunition and reloading tools. Now, tell me what you're going to do about this nighthound business."

Tortha Karf was silent for a while, after Verkan Vall had finished.

"You're taking some awful chances, Vall," he said, at length. "The way you plan doing it, the advantages will all be with the nighthound. Those things can see as well at night as you can in daylight. I suppose you know that, though; you're the nighthound specialist, now."

"Yes. But they're accustomed to the Venus hotland marshes; it's been dry weather for the last two weeks, all over the northeastern section of the Northern Continent. I'll be able to hear it, long before it gets close to me. And I'll be wearing an electric headlamp. When I snap that on, it'll be dazzled, for a moment."

"Well, as I said, you're the nighthound specialist. There's the communicator; order anything you need." He lit a fresh cigarette from the end of the old one before crushing it out. "But be careful, Vall. It took me close to forty years to make a paratimer out of you; I don't want to have to repeat the process with somebody else before I can retire."

The grass was wet as Verkan Vall—who reminded himself that here he was called Richard Lee—crossed the yard from the farmhouse to the ramshackle barn, in the early autumn darkness. It had been raining that morning when the strato-rocket from Dhergabar had landed him at the Hagraban Synthetics Works, on the First Level; unaffected by the probabilities of human history, the same rain had been coming down on the old Kinchwalter farm, near Rutter's Fort, on the Fourth Level. And it had persisted all day.

He didn't like that. The woods would be wet, muffling

his quarry's footsteps, and canceling his only advantage over the night-prowler he hunted. He had no idea, however, of postponing the hunt. If anything, the rain had made it all the more imperative that the nighthound be killed at once. At this season, a falling temperature would speedily follow. The nighthound, a creature of the hot Venus marshes, would suffer from the cold, and, taught by years of domestication to find warmth among human habitations, it would invade some isolated farmhouse, or, worse, one of the little valley villages. If it were not killed tonight, the incident he had come to prevent would certainly occur.

Going to the barn, he spread an old horse blanket on the seat of the jeep, laid his rifle on it, and then backed the jeep outside. Then he took off his coat, removing his pipe and tobacco from the pockets, and, spread it on the wet grass. He unwrapped a package and took out a small plastic spray-gun he had brought with him from the First Level, aiming it at the coat and pressing the trigger until it blew itself empty. A sickening, rancid fetor tainted the air—the scent of the giant poison roach of Venus, the one creature for which the nighthound bore an inborn, implacable hatred. It was because of this compulsive urge to attack and kill the deadly poison roach that the first human settlers on Venus, long millennia ago, had domesticated the ugly and savage nighthound. He remembered that the Gavran family derived their title from their vast Venus hotlands estates; that Gavran Sarn, the man who had brought this thing to the Fourth Level, had been born on the inner planet. When Verkan Vall donned that coat, he would become his own living bait for the murderous fury of the creature he sought. At the moment, mastering his queasiness and putting on the coat, he objected less to that danger than to the hideous stench of the scent, to obtain which a valuable specimen had been sacrificed at the Dhergabar Museum of Extraterrestrial Zoology, the evening before.

Carrying the wrapper and the spray gun to an outside fireplace, he snapped his lighter to them and tossed them in. They were highly inflammable, blazing up and vanishing in a moment. He tested the electric headlamp on the front of his cap; checked his rifle; drew the heavy revolver, an authentic product of his line of operation, and flipped the cylinder out and in again. Then he got into the jeep and drove away.

For half an hour, he drove quickly along the valley roads. Now and then, he passed farmhouses, and dogs, puzzled and angered by the alien scent his coat bore, barked curiously. At length, he turned into a back road, and from this to the barely discernible trace of an old log road. The rain had stopped, and, in order to be ready to fire in any direction at any time, he had removed the top of the jeep. Now he had to crouch below the windshield to avoid overhanging branches. Once, three deer—a buck and two does—stopped in front of him and stared for a moment, then bounded away with a flutter of white tails.

He was driving slowly, now; spraying behind him a reeking trail of scent. There had been another stock killing the night before, while he had been on the First Level. The locality of this latest depredation had confirmed his estimate of the beast's probable movements, and indicated where it might be prowling tonight. He was certain that it was somewhere near; sooner or later, it would pick up the scent.

Finally, he stopped, snapping out his lights. He had chosen this spot carefully, while studying the Geological Survey map, that afternoon; he was on the grade of an old railroad line, now abandoned and its track long removed, which had served the logging operations of fifty years ago. On one side, the mountain slanted sharply upward; on the other, it fell away sharply. If the nighthound were below him, it would have to climb that forty-five degree slope, and could not avoid dislodging loose stones, or otherwise making a noise. He would get out on that side; if the nighthound were above him, the jeep would protect him when it charged. He got to the ground, thumbing off the safety of his rifle, and an instant later he knew that he had made a mistake which could easily cost him his life; a mistake from which neither his comprehensive logic nor his hypnotically acquired knowledge of the beast's habits had saved him.

As he stepped to the ground, facing toward the front of the jeep, he heard a low, whining cry behind him, and a rush of padded feet. He whirled, snapping on the headlamp with his left hand and thrusting out his rifle pistol-wise in his right. For a split second, he saw the charging animal, its long, lizard-like head split in a toothy grin, its talon-tipped forepaws extended.

He fired, and the bullet went wild. The next instant, the rifle was knocked from his hand. Instinctively, he flung up his left arm to shield his eyes. Claws raked his left arm and shoulder, something struck him heavily along the left side, and his cap-light went out as he dropped and rolled under the jeep, drawing in his legs and fumbling under his coat for the revolver.

In that instant, he knew what had gone wrong. His plan had been entirely too much of a success. The nighthound had winded him as he had driven up the old railroad grade, and had followed. Its best running speed had been just good enough to keep it a hundred or so feet behind the jeep, and the motor noise had covered the padding of its feet. In the few moments between stopping the little car and getting out, the nighthound had been able to close the distance and spring upon him.

It was characteristic of First Level mentality that Verkan Vall wasted no moments on self-reproach or panic. While he was still rolling under his jeep, his mind had been busy with plans to retrieve the situation. Something touched the heel of one boot, and he froze his leg into immobility, at the same time trying to get the big Smith & Wesson free. The shoulder holster, he found, was badly torn, though made of the heaviest skirting leather, and the spring which retained the weapon in place had been wrenched and bent until he needed both hands to draw. The eight-inch slashing claw of the nighthound's right intermediary limb had raked him; only the instinctive motion of throwing up his arm, and the fact that he wore the revolver in a shoulder holster, had saved his life.

The nighthound was prowling around the jeep, whining frantically. It was badly confused. It could see quite well, even in the close darkness of the starless night; its eyes were of a nature capable of perceiving infrared radiations as light. There were plenty of these; the jeep's engine, lately running on four-wheel drive, was quite hot. Had he been standing alone, especially on this raw, chilly night, Verkan Vall's own body heat would have lighted him up like a jack-o'-lantern. Now, however, the hot engine above him masked his own radiations. Moreover, the poison roach scect on his coat was coming up through the floor board and mingling with the scent on the seat, yet the nighthound couldn't find the two-

and-a-half foot insectlike thing that should have been producing it. Verkan Vall lay motionless, wondering how long the next move would be in coming. Then he heard a thud above him, followed by a furious tearing as the nighthound ripped the blanket and began rending at the seat cushion.

"Hope it gets a paw full of seat springs," Verkan Vall commented mentally. He had already found a stone about the size of his two fists, and another slightly smaller, and had put one in each of the side pockets of the coat. Now he slipped his revolver into his waist-belt and writhed out of the coat, shedding the ruined shoulder holster at the same time. Wriggling on the flat of his back, he squirmed between the rear wheels, until he was able to sit up, behind the jeep. Then, swinging the weighted coat, he flung it forward, over the nighthound and the jeep itself, at the same time drawing his revolver.

Immediately, the nighthound, lured by the sudden movement of the principal source of the scent, jumped out of the jeep and bounded after the coat, and there was considerable noise in the brush on the lower side of the railroad grade. At once, Verkan Vall swarmed into the jeep and snapped on the lights.

His stratagem had succeeded beautifully. The stinking coat had landed on the top of a small bush, about ten feet in front of the jeep and ten feet from the ground. The nighthound, erect on its haunches, was reaching out with its front paws to drag it down, and slashing angrily at it with its single clawed intermediary limb. Its back was to Verkan Vall.

His sights clearly defined by the lights in front of him, the paratimer centered them on the base of the creature's spine, just above its secondary shoulders, and carefully squeezed the trigger. The big .357 Magnum bucked in his hand and belched flame and sound—if only these Fourth

Level weapons weren't so confoundedly boisterous!—and the nighthound screamed and fell. Recocking the revolver, Verkan Vall waited for an instant, then nodded in satisfaction. The beast's spine had been smashed, and its hind quarters, and even its intermediary fighting limbs had been paralyzed. He aimed carefully for a second shot and fired into the base of the thing's skull. It quivered and died.

Getting a flashlight, he found his rifle, sticking muzzle down in the mud a little behind and to the right of the jeep, and swore briefly in the local Fourth Level idiom, for Verkan Vall was a man who loved good weapons, be they sigma-ray needlers, neutron-disruption blasters, or the solid-missile projectors of the lower levels. By this time, he was feeling considerable pain from the claw wounds he had received. He peeled off his shirt and tossed it over the hood of the jeep.

Tortha Karf had advised him to carry a needler, or a blaster, or a neurostat-gun, but Verkan Vall had been unwilling to take such arms onto the Fourth Level. In event of mishap to himself, it would be all too easy for such a weapon to fall into the hands of someone able to deduce from it scientific principles too far in advance of the general Fourth Level culture. But there had been one First Level item which he had permitted himself, mainly because, suitably packaged, it was not readily identifiable as such. Digging a respectable Fourth Level leatherette case from under the seat, he opened it and took out a pint bottle with a red poison label, and a towel. Saturating the towel with the contents of the bottle, he rubbed every inch of his torso with it, so as not to miss even the smallest break made in his skin by the septic claws of the nighthound. Whenever the lotion-soaked towel touched raw skin, a pain like the burn of a hot iron shot through him; before he was through, he was in agony. Satisfied that he had disinfected every wound, he dropped the towel and clung weakly to the side of the jeep. He grunted out a string of English oaths, and capped them with an obscene Spanish blasphemy he had picked up among the Fourth Level inhabitants of his island home of Nerros, to the south, and a thundering curse in the name of Mogga, Fire-God of Dool, in a Third-Level tongue. He mentioned Fasif, Great God of Khift, in a manner which would have got him an acid-bath if the Khiftan priests had heard him. He alluded to the baroque amatory practices of the Third-Level Illyalla people, and soothed himself, in the classical Dar-Halma tongue, with one of those rambling genealogical insults favored in the Indo-Turanian Sector of the Fourth Level.

By this time, the pain had subsided to an over-all smarting itch. He'd have to bear with that until his work was finished and he could enjoy a hot bath. He got another bottle out of the first-aid kit—a flat pint, labeled "Old Overholt," containing a locally-manufactured specific for inward and subjective wounds—and medicated himself copiously from it, corking it and slipping it into his hip pocket against future need. He gathered up the ruined shoulder-holster and threw it under the back seat. He put on his shirt. Then he went and dragged the dead nighthound onto the grade by its stumpy tail.

It was an ugly thing, weighing close to two hundred pounds, with powerfully muscled hind legs which furnished the bulk of its motive-power, and sturdy three-clawed front legs. Its secondary limbs, about a third of the way back from its front shoulders, were long and slender; normally, they were carried folded closely against the body, and each was armed with a single curving claw. The revolver-bullet had gone in at the base of the skull and emerged under the jaw; the head was relatively undamaged. Verkan Vall was glad of that; he wanted that head for the trophy-room of his home on Nerros. Grunting and straining, he got the thing into the back of the jeep, and flung his almost shredded tweed coat over it.

A last look around assured him that he had left nothing unaccountable or suspicious. The brush was broken where the nighthound had been tearing at the coat; a bear might have done that. There ware splashes of the viscid stuff the thing had used for blood, but they wouldn't be there long. Terrestrial rodents liked nighthound blood, and the woods were full of mice. He climbed in under the wheel, backed, turned, and drove away.

Inside the paratime-transposition dome, Verkan Vall turned from the body of the nighthound, which he had just dragged in, and considered the inert form of another animal—a stump-tailed, tuft-eared tawny Canada lynx. That particular animal had already made two paratime-transpositions; captured in the vast wilderness of Fifth-Level North America, it had been taken to the First Level and placed in the Dhergabar Zoological Gardens, and then requisitioned on the authority of Tortha Karf, it had been brought to the Fourth Level by Varkan Vall. It was almost at the end of its travels.

Verkan Vall prodded the supine animal with the toe of his boot; it twitched slightly. Its feet were cross-bound with straps, but when he saw that the narcotic was wearing off, Verkan Vall snatched a syringe, parted the fur at the base of its neck, and gave it an injection. After a moment, he picked it up in his arms and carried it out to the jeep.

"All right, pussy cat," he said, placing it under the rear seat, "this is the one-way ride. The way you're doped up, it won't hurt a bit."

He went back and rummaged in the debris of the long-deserted barn. He picked up a hoe, and discarded it as too light. An old plowshare was too unhandy. He considered a grate-bar from a heating furnace, and then he found the poleax, lying among a pile of wormeaten boards. Its handle had been shortened, at some time, to about twelve inches, converting it into a heavy hatchet. He weighed it, and tried it on a block of wood, and then, making sure that the secret door was closed, he went out again and drove off.

An hour later, he returned. Opening the secret door, he carried the ruined shoulder holster, and the straps that had bound the bobcat's feet, and the ax, now splotched with blood and tawny cat-hairs, into the dome. Then he closed the secret room, and took a long drink from the bottle on his hip.

The job was done. He would take a hot bath, and sleep in the farmhouse till noon, and then he would return to the First Level. Maybe Tortha Karf would want him to come back here for a while. The situation on this time-line was far from satisfactory, even if the crisis threatened by Gavran Sarn's renegade pet had been averted. The presence of a chief's assistant might be desirable.

At least, he had a right to expect a short vacation. He thought of the little redhead at the Hagraban Synthetics Works. What was her name? Something Kara—Morvan Kara; that was it. She'd be coming off shift about the time he'd make First Level, tomorrow afternoon.

The claw-wounds were still smarting vexatiously. A hot bath, and a night's sleep— He took another drink, lit his pipe, picked up his rifle and started across the yard to the house.

Private Zinkowski cradled the telephone and got up from the desk, stretching. He left the orderly-room and walked across the hall to the recreation room, where the rest of the boys were loafing. Sergeant Haines, in a languid gin-rummy game with Corporal Conner, a sheriff's deputy, and a mechanic from the service station down the road, looked up.

"Well, Sarge, I think we can write off those stock-killings," the private said.

"Yeah?" The sergeant's interest quickened.

"Yeah. I think the whatzit's had it. I just got a buzz from the railroad cops at Logansport. It seems a track-walker found a dead bobcat on the Logan River branch, about a mile or so below MMY signal tower. Looks like it tangled with that night freight up-river, and came off second best. It was near chopped to hamburger."

"MMY signal tower; that's right below Yoder's Crossing," the sergeant considered. "The Strawmyer farm night-before-last, the Amrine farm last night— Yeah, that would be about right."

"That'll suit Steve Parker; bobcats aren't protected, so it's not his trouble. And they're not a violation of state law, so it's none of our worry," Conner said. "Your deal, isn't it, Sarge?"

"Yeah. Wait a minute." The sergeant got to his feet. "I promised Sam Kane, the AP man at Logansport, that I'd let him in on anything new." He got up and started for the phone. "Phantom Killer!" He blew an impolite noise.

"Well, it was a lot of excitement, while it lasted," the deputy sheriff said. "Just like that Flying Saucer thing."

It's always hard for one race to understand an utterly alien one. The Encyclopedia, for instance, got his knowledge from a robot—and missed one vital factor!

# Ogre

**By Clifford D. Simak**

Illustrated by Kramer

The moss brought the news. Hundreds of miles the word had gossiped its way along, through many devious ways. For the moss did not grow everywhere. It grew only where the soil was sparse and niggardly, where the larger, lustier, more vicious plant things could not grow to rob it of light or uproot it, or crowd it out, or do it other harm.

The moss told the story to Nicodemus, life blanket of Don Mackenzie, and it all came about because Mackenzie took a bath.

Mackenzie took his time in the bathroom, wallowing around in the tub and braying out a song, while Nicodemus, feeling only half a thing, moped outside the door. Without Mackenzie, Nicodemus was, in fact, even less than half a thing. Accepted as intelligent life, Nicodemus and others of his tribe were intelligent only when they were wrapped about their humans. Their intelligence and emotions were borrowed from the things that wore them.

For the aeons before the human beings came to this twilight world, the life blankets had dragged out a humdrum existence. Occasionally one of them allied itself with a higher form of plant life, but not often. After all, such an arrangement was very little better than staying as they were.

When the humans came, however, the blankets finally clicked. Between them and the men of Earth grew up a perfect mutual agreement, a highly profitable and agreeable instance of symbiosis. Overnight, the blankets became one of the greatest single factors in galactic exploration

For the man who wore one of them, like a cloak around his shoulders, need never worry where a meal was coming from; knew, furthermore, that he would be fed correctly, with a scientific precision that automically counterbalanced any upset of metabolism that might be brought by alien conditions. For the curious plants had the ability to gather energy and convert it into food for the human body, had an uncanny instinct as to the exact needs of the body, extending, to a limited extent, to certain basic medical requirements.

But if the life blankets gave men food and warmth, served as a family doctor, man lent them something that was even more precious—the consciousness of life. The moment one of the plants wrapped itself around a man it became, in a sense, the double of that man. It shared his intelligence and emotions, was whisked from the dreary round of its own existence into a more exalted pseudo-life.

# OGRE

Nicodemus, at first moping outside the bathroom door, gradually grew peeved. He felt his thin veneer of human life slowly ebbing from him and he was filled with a baffling resentment.

Finally, feeling very put upon, he waddled out of the trading post upon his own high lonesome, flapping awkwardly along, like a sheet billowing in the breeze.

The dull brick-red sun that was Sigma Draco shone down upon a world that even at high noon appeared to be in twilight and Nicodemus' bobbling shape cast squirming, unsubstantial purple shadows upon the green and crimson gound. A rifle tree took a shot at Nicodemus but missed him by a yard at least. That tree had been off the beam for weeks. It had missed everything it shot at. Its best effort had been scaring the life out of Nellie, the bookkeeping robot that never told a lie, when it banked one of its bulletlike seeds against the steel-sheeted post.

But no one had felt very badly about that, for no one cared for Nellie. With Nellie around, no one could chisel a red cent off the company. That, incidentally, was the reason she was at the post.

But for a couple of weeks now, Nellie hadn't bothered anybody. She had taken to chumming around with Encyclopedia, who more than likely was slowly going insane trying to figure out her thoughts.

Nicodemus told the rifle tree what he thought of it, shooting at its own flesh and blood, as it were, and kept shuffling along. The tree, knowing Nicodemus for a traitor to his own, a vegetable renegade, took another shot at him, missed by two yards and gave up in disgust.

That is how he heard that Alder, a minor musician out in

Melody Bowl, finally had achieved a masterpiece. Nicodemus knew it might have happened weeks before, for Melody Bowl was half a world away and the news sometimes had to travel the long way around, but just the same he scampered as fast as he could hump back toward the post.

For this was news that couldn't wait. This was news Mackenzie had to know at once. He managed to kick up quite a cloud of dust coming down the home stretch and flapped triumphantly through the door, above which hung the crudely lettered sign:

GALACTIC TRADING CO.

Just what good the sign did, no one yet had figured out. The humans were the only living things on the planet that could read it.

Before the bathroom door, Nicodemus reared up and beat his fluttering self against it with tempetuous urgency.

"All right," yelled Mackenzie. "All right. I know I took too long again. Just calm yourself. I'll be right out."

Nicodemus settled down but, still wriggling with the news he had to tell, heard Mackenzie swabbing out the tub.

With Nicodemus wrapped happily about him, Mackenzie strode into the office and found Nelson Harper, the factor, with his feet up on the desk, smoking his pipe and studying the ceiling.

"Howdy, lad," said the factor. He pointed at a bottle with his pipestem. "Grab yourself a snort."

Mackenzie grabbed one.

"Nicodemus has been out chewing fat with the moss," he said. "Tells me a conductor by the name Alder has composed a symphony. Moss says it's a masterpiece."

Harper took his feet off the desk. Never heard of this chap, Alder," he said.

"Never heard of Kadmar, either," Mackenzie reminded him, "until he produced the Red Sun symphony. Now everyone is batty over him.

"If Alder has anything at all, we ought to get it down. Even a mediocre piece pays out. People back on Earth are plain wacky over this tree music of ours. Like that one fellow . . . that composer— "

"Wade," Harper filled in. "J. Edgerton Wade. One of the greatest composers Earth had ever known. Quit in mortification after he heard the Red Sun piece. Later disappeared. No one knows where he went."

The factor nursed his pipe between his palms. "Funny thing. Came out here figuring our best-grading bet would be new drugs or maybe some new kind of food. Something for the high-class restaurants to feature, charge ten bucks a plate for. Maybe even a new mineral. Like out on Eta Cassiop. But it wasn't any of those things. It was music. Symphony stuff. High-brow racket."

Mackenzie took another shot at the bottle, put it back and wiped his mouth. "I'm not so sure I like this music angle," he declared. "I don't know much about music. But it sounds funny to me, what I've heard of it. Brain-twisting stuff."

Harper grunted. "You're O.K. as long as you have plenty of serum along. If you can't take the music, just keep yourself shot full of serum. That way it can't touch you."

Mackenzie nodded. "It almost got Alexander that time, remember? Ran short on serum while he was down in the

Bowl trying to dicker with the trees. Music seemed to have a hold on him. He didn't want to leave. He fought and screeched and yelled around . . . I felt like a heel, taking him away. He never has been quite the same since then. Doctors back on Earth finally were able to get him straightened out, but warned him never to come back."

"He's back again," said Harper, quietly

"Alexander's back again," said Harper. "Grant spotted him over at the Groombridge post. Throwing in with the Groomies, I guess. Just a yellow-bellied renegade. Going against his own race. You boys shouldn't have saved him that time. Should have let the music get him."

"What are you going to do about it?" demanded Mackenzie.

Harper shrugged his shoulders. "What can I do about it? Unless I want to declare war on the Groombridge post. And that is out. Haven't you heard it's all sweetness and light between Earth and Groombridge 34? That's the reason the two posts are stuck away from Melody Bowl. So each one of us will have a fair shot at the music. All according to some pact the two companies rigged up. Galactic's got so pure they wouldn't even like it if they knew we had a spy planted on the Groomie post."

"But they got one planted on us," declared Mackenzie. "We haven't been able to find him, of course, but we know there is one. He's out there in the woods somewhere, watching every move we make."

Harper nodded his head. "You can't trust a Groomie. The lousy little insects will stoop to anything. They don't want that music, can't use it. Probably don't even know what music is. Haven't any hearing. But they know Earth wants it, will pay any price to get it, so they are out here to beat us to it. They work through birds like Alexander. They get the stuff, Alexander peddles it."

"What if we run across Alexander, chief?"

Harper clicked his pipestem across his teeth. "Depends on circumstances. Try to hire him, maybe. Get him away from the Groomies. He's a good trader. The company would do right by him."

Mackenzie shook his head. "No soap. He hates Galactic. Something that happened years ago. He'd rather make us trouble than turn a good deal for himself."

"Maybe he's changed," suggested Harper. "Maybe you boys saving him changed his mind."

"I don't think it did," persisted Mackenzie.

The factor reached across the desk and drew a humidor in front of him, began to refill his pipe.

"Been trying to study out something else, too," he said. "Wondering what to do with the Encyclopedia. He wants to go to Earth. Seems he's found out just enough from us to whet his appetite for knowledge. Says he wants to go to Earth and study our civilization."

Mackenzie grimaced. "That baby's gone through our minds with a fine-toothed comb. He knows some of the things we've forgotten we ever knew. I guess it's just the nature of him, but it gets my wind up when I think of it."

"He's after Nellie now," said Harper. "Trying to untangle what she knows."

"It would serve him right if he found out."

"I've been trying to figure it out," said Harper. "I don't like this brain-picking of his any more than you do, but if we took him to Earth, away from his own stamping grounds, we might be able to soften him up. He certainly knows a lot about this planet that would be of value to us. He's told me a little— "

"Don't fool yourself," said Mackenzie. "He hasn't told you a thing more than he's had to tell to make you believe it wasn't a one-way deal. Whatever he has told you has no vital significance. Don't kid yourself, he'll exchange information for information. That cookie's out to get everything he can get for nothing."

The factor regarded Mackenzie narrowly. "I'm not sure but I should put you in for an Earth vacation," he declared. "You're letting things upset you. You're losing your perspective. Alien planets aren't Earth, you know. You have to expect wacky things, get along with them, accept them on the basis of the logic that makes them the way they are."

"I know all that," agreed Mackenzie, "but honest, chief, this place gets in my hair at times. Trees that shoot at you, moss that talks, vines that heave thunderbolts at you—and now, the Encyclopedia."

"The Encyclopedia is logical," insisted Harper. "He's a repository for knowledge. We have parallels on Earth. Men who study merely for the sake of learning, never expect to use the knowledge they amass. They derive a strange, smug satisfaction from being well informed. Combine that yearning for knowledge with a phenomenal ability to memorize and co-ordinate that knowledge and you have the Encyclopedia."

"But there must be a purpose to him," insisted Mackenzie. "There must be some reason back of this thirst for knowledge. Just soaking up facts doesn't add up to anything unless you use those facts."

Harper puffed stolidly at his pipe. "There may be a purpose in it, but a purpose so deep, so different, we could not recognize it. This planet is a vegetable world and a vegetable civilization. Back on earth the animals got the head start and plants never had a chance to learn or to evolve. But here it's a different story. The plants were the ones that evolved, became masters of the situation."

"If there is a purpose, we should know it," Mackenzie declared, stubbornly. "We can't afford to go blind on a thing like this. If the Encyclopedia has a game, we should know it. Is he acting on his own, a free lance? Or is he the representative of the world, a sort of prime minister, a state department? Or is he something that was left over by another civilization, a civilization that is gone? A kind of living archive of knowledge, still working at his old trade even if the need of it is gone?"

"You worry too much," Harper told him.

"We have to worry, chief. We can't afford to let anything get ahead of us. We have taken the attitude we're superior to this vegetable civilization, if you can call it a civilization, that has developed here. It's the logical attitude to take because nettles and dandelions and trees aren't anything to be afraid of back home. But what holds on Earth doesn't hold here. We have to ask ourselves what a vegetable civilization would be like. What would it want? What would be its aspirations and how would it go about realizing them?"

"We're getting off the subject," said Harper, curtly. "You came in here to tell me about some new symphony."

Mackenzie flipped his hands. "O. K. if that's the way you feel about it."

"Maybe we better figure on grabbing up this symphony soon as we can," said Harper. "We haven't had a really good one since the Red Sun. And if we mess around, the Groomies will beat us to it."

"Maybe they have already," said Mackenzie.

Harper puffed complacently at his pipe. "They haven't done it yet. Grant keeps me posted on every move they make. He doesn't miss a thing that happens at the Groombridge post."

"Just the same," declared Mackenzie, "we can't go rushing off and tip our hand. The Groomie spy isn't asleep, either."

"Got any ideas?" asked the factor.

"We could take the ground car," suggested Mackenzie. "It's slower than the flier, but if we took the flier the Groomie would know there was something up. We use the car a dozen times a day. He'd think nothing of it."

Harper considered. "The idea has merit, lad. Who would you take?"

"Let me have Brad Smith," said Mackenzie. "We'll get along all right, just the two of us. He's an old-timer out here. Knows his way around."

Harper nodded. "Better take Nellie, too."

"Not on your life!" yelped Mackenzie. "What do you want to do? Get rid of her so you can make a cleaning?"

Harper wagged his grizzled head sadly. "Good idea, but it can't be did. One cent off and she's on your trail. Use to be a little graft a fellow could pick up here and there, but not any more. Not since they got those robot bookkeepers indoctrinated with truth and honesty."

"I won't take her," Mackenzie declared, flatly. "So help me, I won't. She'll spout company law all the way there and back. With the crush she has on this Encyclopedia, she'll probably want to drag him along, too. We'll have trouble enough with rifle trees and electro vines and all the other crazy vegetables without having an educated cabbage and a tin-can lawyer underfoot."

"You've got to take her," insisted Harper, mildly. "New ruling. Got to have one of the things along on every deal you make to prove you did right by the natives. Come right down to it, the ruling probably is your own fault. If you hadn't been so foxy on that Red Sun deal, the company never would have thought of it."

"All I did was to save the company some money," protested Mackenzie.

"You knew," Harper reminded him crisply, "that the standard price for a symphony is two bushels of fertilizer. Why did you have to chisel half a bushel on Kadmar?"

"Cripes," said Mackenzie, "Kadmar didn't know the difference. He practically kissed me for a bushel and a half."

"That's not the point," declared Harper. "The company's got the idea we got to shoot square with everything we trade with, even if it's nothing but a tree."

"I know," said Mackenzie, dryly. "I've read the manual."

"Just the same," said Harper, "Nellie goes along."

He studied Mackenzie over the bowl of his pipe.

"Just to be sure you don't forget again," he said.

The man who back on Earth had been known as J. Edgerton Wade, crouched on the low cliff that dropped away into Melody Bowl. The dull red sun was slipping toward the purple horizon and soon, Wade knew, the trees would play their regular evening concert. He hoped that once again it would be the wondrous new symphony Alder had composed.

Thinking about it, he shuddered in ecstasy—shuddered again when he thought about the setting sun. The evening chill would be coming soon.

Wade had no life blanket. His food, cached back in the tiny cave in the cliff, was nearly gone. His ship, smashed in his inexpert landing on the planet almost a year before, was a rusty hulk. J. Edgerton Wade was near the end of his rope—and knew it. Strangely, he didn't care. In that year since he'd come here to the cliffs, he'd lived in a world of beauty. Evening after evening he had listened to the concerts. That was enough, he told himself. After a year of music such as that any man could afford to die.

He swept his eyes up and down the little valley that made up the Bowl, saw the trees set in orderly rows, almost as if someone had planted them. Some intelligence that may at one time, long ago, have squatted on this very cliff edge, even as he squatted now, and listened to the music.

But there was no evidence, he knew, to support such a hypothesis. No ruins of cities had been found upon this world. No evidence that any civilization, in the sense that Earth had built a civilization, ever had existed here. Nothing at all that suggested a civilized race had ever laid eyes upon this valley, had ever had a thing to do with the planning of the bowl.

Nothing, that was, except the cryptic messages on the face of the cliff above the cave where he cached his food and slept. Scrawlings that bore no resemblance to any other writing Wade had ever seen. Perhaps, he speculated, they might have been made by other aliens who, like himself, had come to listen to the music until death had come for them.

Still crouching, Wade rocked slowly on the balls of his feet. Perhaps he should scrawl his own name there with the other scrawlings. Like one would sign a hotel register. A lonely name scratched upon the face of a lonely rock. A grave name, a brief memorial—and yet it would be the only tombstone he would ever have.

The music would be starting soon and then he would forget about the cave, about the food that was almost gone, about the rusting ship that never could carry him back to Earth again—even had he wanted to go back. And he didn't—he couldn't have gone back. The Bowl had trapped him, the music had spun a web about him. Without it, he knew, he could not live. It had become a part of him. Take it from him and he would be a shell, for it was now a part of the life force that surged within his body, part of his brain and blood, a silvery thread of meaning that ran through his thoughts and purpose.

The trees stood in quiet, orderly ranks and beside each tree was a tiny mound, podia for the conductors, and beside each mound the dark mouths of burrows. The conductors, Wade knew, were in those burrows, resting for the concert. Being animals, the conductors had to get their rest.

But the trees never needed rest. They never slept. They never tired, these gray, drab music trees, the trees that sang to the empty sky, sang of forgotten days and days that had not come, of days when Sigma Draco had been a mighty sun and of the later days when it would be a cinder circling in space. And of other things an Earthman could never know, could only sense and strain toward and wish he knew. Things that stirred strange thoughts within one's brain and choked one with alien emotion an Earthman was never meant to feel. Emotion and thought that one could not even recognize, yet emotion and thought that one yearned toward and knew never could be caught.

## OGRE

Technically, of course, it wasn't the trees that sang. Wade knew that, but he did not think about it often. He would rather it had been the trees alone. He seldom thought of the music other than belonging to the trees and disregarded the little entities inside the trees that really made the music, using the trees for their sounding boards. Entities? That was all he knew. Insects, perhaps, a colony of insects to each tree—or maybe even nymphs or sprites or some of the other little folks that run on skipping feet through the pages of children's fairy books. Although that was foolish, he told himself—there were no sprites.

Each insect, each sprite contributing its own small part to the orchestration, compliant to the thought-vibrations of the conductors. The conductors thought the music, held it in their brains and the things in the trees responded.

It didn't sound so pretty that way, Wade told himself. Thinking it out spoiled the beauty of it. Better to simply accept it and enjoy it without explanation.

Men came at times—not often—men of his own flesh and blood, men from the trading post somewhere on the planet. They came to record the music and then they went away. How anyone could go away once they had heard the music, Wade could not understand. Faintly he remembered there was a way one could immunize one's self against the music's spell, condition one's self so he could leave after he had heard it, dull his senses to a point where it could not hold him. Wade shivered at the thought. That was sacrilege. But still no worse than recording the music so Earth orchestras might play it. For what Earth orchestra could play it as he heard it here, evening after evening? If Earth music lovers only could hear it as it was played here in this ancient bowl!

When the Earthmen came, Wade always hid. It would

be just like them to try to take him back with them, away from the music of the trees.

Faintly the evening breeze brought the foreign sound to him, the sound that should not have been heard there in the Bowl—the clank of steel on stone.

Rising from his squatting place, he tried to locate the origin of the sound. It came again, from the far edge of the Bowl. He shielded his eyes with a hand against the setting sun, stared across the Bowl at the moving figures.

There were three of them and one, he saw at once, was an Earthman. The other two were strange creatures that looked remotely like monster bugs, chitinous armor glinting in the last rays of Sigma Draco. Their heads, he saw, resembled grinning skulls and they wore dark harnesses, apparently for the carrying of tools or weapons.

Groombridgians! But what would Groombridgians be doing with an Earthman? The two were deadly trade rivals, were not above waging intermittent warfare when their interests collided.

Something flashed in the sun—a gleaming tool that stabbed and probed, stabbed and lifted.

J. Edgerton Wade froze in horror.

Such a thing, he told himself, simply couldn't happen!

The three across the Bowl were digging up a music tree!

The vine sneaked through the rustling sea of grass, cautious tendrils raised to keep tab on its prey, the queer, clanking thing that still rolled on unswervingly. Came on without stopping to smell out the ground ahead, without zigzagging to throw off possible attack.

Its action was puzzling; that was no way for anything to travel on this planet. For a moment a sense of doubt trilled

along the length of vine, doubt of the wisdom of attacking anything that seemed so sure. But the doubt was short lived, driven out by the slavering anticipation that had sent the vicious vegetable from its lair among the grove of rifle trees. The vine trembled a little—slightly drunk with the vibration that pulsed through its tendrils.

The queer thing rumbled on and the vine tensed itself, every fiber alert for struggle. Just let it get so much as one slight grip upon the thing—

The prey came closer and for one sense-shattering moment it seemed it would be out of reach. Then it lurched slightly to one side as it struck a hump in the ground and the vine's tip reached out and grasped, secured a hold, wound itself in a maddened grip and hauled, hauled with all the might of almost a quarter mile of trailing power.

Inside the ground car, Don Mackenzie felt the machine lurch sickeningly, kicked up the power and spun the tractor on its churning treads in an effort to break loose.

Back of him Bradford Smith uttered a startled whoop and dived for an energy gun that had broken from its rack and was skidding across the floor. Nellie, upset by the lurch, was flat on her back, jammed into a corner. The Encyclopedia, at the moment of shock, had whipped out its coiled-up taproot and tied up to a pipe. Now, like an anchored turtle, it swayed pendulum-wise across the floor.

Glass tinkled and metal screeched on metal as Nellie thrashed to regain her feet. The ground car reared and seemed to paw the air, slid about and plowed great furrows in the ground.

"It's a vine!" shrieked Smith.

Mackenzie nodded, grim-lipped, fighting the wheel. As the car slewed around, he saw the arcing loops of the attacker, reaching from the grove of rifle trees. Something pinged against the vision plate, shattered into a puff of dust. The rifle trees were limbering up.

Mackenzie tramped on the power, swung the car in a wide circle, giving the vine some slack, then quartered and charged across the prairie while the vine twisted and flailed the air in looping madness. If only he could build up speed, slap into the stretched-out vine full tilt, Mackenzie was sure he could break its hold. In a straight pull, escape would have been hopeless, for the vine, once fastened on the thing, was no less than a steel cable of strength and determination.

Smith had managed to get a port open, was trying to shoot, the energy gun crackling weirdly. The car rocked from side to side, gaining speed while bulletlike seeds from the rifle trees pinged and whined against it.

Mackenzie braced himself and yelled at Smith. They must be nearing the end of their run. Any minute now would come the jolt as they rammed into the tension of the outstretched vine.

It came with terrifying suddenness, a rending thud. Instinctively, Mackenzie threw up his arms to protect himself, for one startled moment knew he was being hurled into the vision plate. A gigantic burst of flame flared in his head and filled the universe. Then he was floating through darkness that was cool and soft and he found himself thinking that everything would be all right, everything would be . . . everything—

But everything wasn't all right. He knew that, the moment he opened his eyes and stared up into the mass of tangled wreckage that hung above him. For many seconds he did not move, did not even wonder where he was. Then he stirred and a piece of steel bit into his leg. Carefully he slid his leg upward, clearing it of the steel. Cloth ripped with an angry snarl, but his leg came free.

"Lie still, you lug," something said, almost as if it were a voice from inside him.

Mackenzie chuckled. "So you're all right," he said.

"Sure. I'm all right," said Nicodemus. "But you got some bruises and a scratch or two and you're liable to have a headache if you—"

The voice trailed off and stopped. Nicodemus was busy. At the moment, he was the medicine cabinet, fashioning from pure energy those things that a man needed when he had a bruise or two and was scratched-up some and might have a headache later.

Mackenzie lay on his back and stared up at the mass of tangled wreckage.

"Wonder how we'll get out of here," he said.

The wreckage above him stirred. A gadget of some sort fell away from the twisted mass and gashed his cheek. He swore—unenthusiastically.

Someone was calling his name and he answered.

The wreckage was jerked about violently, literally torn apart. Long metal arms reached down, gripped him by the shoulders and yanked him out, none too gently.

"Thanks, Nellie," he said.

"Shut up," said Nellie, tartly.

His knees were a bit wobbly and he sat down, staring at the ground car. It didn't look much like a ground car any more. It had smashed full tilt into a boulder and was a mess.

To his left Smith also was sitting on the ground and he was chuckling.

"What's the matter with you," snapped Mackenzie.

"Jerked her right up by the roots," exulted Smith. "So help me, right smack out of the ground. That's one vine that'll never bother anyone again."

Mackenzie stared in amazement. The vine lay coiled on the ground, stretching back toward the grove, limp and dead. Its smaller tendrils still were entwined in the tangled wreckage of the car.

"It hung on," gasped Mackenzie. "We didn't break its hold!"

"Nope," agreed Smith, "we didn't break its hold, but we sure ruined it."

"Lucky thing it wasn't an electro," said Mackenzie, "or it would have fried us."

Smith nodded glumly. "As it is it's loused us up enough. That car will never run again. And us a couple thousand miles from home."

Nellie emerged from a hole in the wreckage, with the Encyclopedia under one arm and a mangled radio under the other. She dumped them both on the ground. The Encyclopedia scuttled off a few feet, drilled his taproot into the soil and was at home.

Nellie glowered at Mackenzie. "I'll report you for this," she declared, vengefully. "The idea of breaking up a nice new car! Do you know what a car costs the company? No, of course, you don't. And you don't care. Just go ahead and break it up. Just like that. Nothing to it. The company's got a lot more money to buy another one. I wonder sometimes if you ever wonder where your pay is coming from. If I was the company, I'd take it out of your salary. Every cent of it, until it was paid for."

Smith eyed Nellie speculatively. "Some day," he said, "I'm going to take a sledge and play tin shinny with you."

"Maybe you got something there," agreed Mackenzie. "There are times when I'm inclined to think the company went just a bit too far in making those robots cost conscious."

"You don't need to talk like that," shrilled Nellie. "Like I was just a machine you didn't need to pay no attention to. I suppose next thing you will be saying it wasn't your fault, that you couldn't help it."

"I kept a good quarter mile from all the groves," growled Mackenzie. "Who ever heard of a vine that could stretch that far?"

"And that ain't all, neither," yelped Nellie. "Smith hit some of the rifle trees."

The two men looked toward the grove. What Nellie said was true. Pale wisps of smoke still rose above the grove and what trees were left looked the worse for wear.

Smith clucked his tongue in mock concern.

"The trees were shooting at us," retorted Mackenzie.

"That don't make any difference," Nellie yelled. "The rule book says—"

Mackenzie waved her into silence. "Yes, I know. Section 17 of the Chapter on Relations with Extraterrestrial Life: *'No employee of this company may employ weapons against or otherwise injure or attempt to injure or threaten with injury an inhabitant of any other planet except in self-defense and then only if every means of escape or settlement has failed.'* "

"And now we got to go back to the post," Nellie shrieked. "When we were almost there, we got to turn back. News of what we did will get around. The moss probably has started already. The idea of ripping a vine up by the roots and shooting trees. If we don't start back right now, we won't get back. Every living thing along the way will be laying for us."

"It was the vine's fault," yelled Smith. "It tried to trap us. It tried to steal our car, probably would have killed us, just for the few lousy ounces of radium we have in the motors. That radium was ours. Not the vine's. It belonged to your beloved company."

"For the love of gosh, don't tell her that," Mackenzie warned, "or she'll go out on a one-robot expedition, yanking vines up left and right."

"Good idea," insisted Smith. "She might tie into an electro. It would peel her paint."

"How about the radio!" Mackenzie asked Nellie.

"Busted," said Nellie, crustily.

"And the recording equipment?"

"The tape's all right and I can fix the recorder."

"Serum jugs busted?"

"One of them ain't," said Nellie.

"O.K., then," said Mackenzie, "get back in there and dig out two bags of fertilizer. We're going on. Melody Bowl is only about fifty miles away."

"We can't do that," protested Nellie. "Every tree will be waiting for us, every vine—"

"It's safer to go ahead than back," said Mackenzie. "Even if we have no radio, Harper will send someone out with the flier to look us up when we are overdue."

He rose slowly and unholstered his pistol.

"Get in there and get that stuff," he ordered. "If you don't, I'll melt you down into a puddle."

"All right," screamed Nellie in sudden terror. "All right. You needn't get so tough about it."

"Any more back talk out of you," Mackenzie warned, "and I'll kick you so full of dents you'll walk stooped over."

They stayed in the open, well away from the groves, keeping a close watch. Mackenzie went ahead and behind him came the Encyclopedia, humping along to keep pace with them. Back of the Encyclopedia was Nellie, loaded down with the bags of fertilizer and equipment. Smith brought up the rear.

A rifle tree took a shot at them, but the range was too far for accurate shooting. Back a way, an electro vine had come closer with a thunderbolt.

Walking was grueling. The grass was thick and matted and one had to plow through it, as if one were walking in water.

"I'll make you sorry for this," seethed Nellie. "I'll make—"

"Shut up," snapped Smith. "For once you're doing a robot's work instead of gumshoeing around to see if you can't catch a nickel out of place."

They breasted a hill and started to climb the long grassy slope.

Suddenly a sound like the savage ripping of a piece of cloth struck across the silence.

They halted, tensed, listening. The sound came again and then again.

"Guns!" yelped Smith.

Swiftly the two men loped up the slope, Nellie galloping awkwardly behind, the bags of fertilizer bouncing on her shoulders.

From the hilltop, Mackenzie took in the situation at a glance.

On the hillside below a man was huddled behind a boulder, working a gun with fumbling desperation, while farther down the hill a ground car had toppled over. Behind the car were three figures—one man and two insect creatures.

"Groomies!" whooped Smith.

A well-directed shot from the car took the top off the boulder and the man behind it hugged the ground.

Smith was racing quarterly down the hill, heading toward another boulder that would outflank the trio at the car.

A yell of human rage came from the car and a bolt from one of the three guns snapped at Smith, plowing a smoking furrow no more than ten feet behind him.

Another shot flared toward Mackenzie and he plunged behind a hummock. A second shot whizzed just above his head and he hunkered down trying to push himself into the ground.

From the slope below came the high-pitched, angry chittering of the Groombridgians.

The car, Mackenzie saw, was not the only vehicle on the hillside. Apparently it had been pulling a trailer to which was lashed a tree. Mackenzie squinted against the setting sun, trying to make out what it was all about. The tree, he saw, had been expertly dug, its roots balled in earth and wrapped in sacking that shone wetly. The trailer was canted at an awkward angle, the treetop sweeping the ground, the balled roots high in the air.

Smith was pouring a deadly fire into the hostile camp and the three below were replying with a sheet of blasting bolts, plowing up the soil around the boulder. In a minute or two, Mackenzie knew, they would literally cut the ground out from under Smith. Cursing under his breath, he edged around the hummock, pushing his pistol before him, wishing he had a rifle.

The third man was slinging an occasional, inexpert shot at the three below, but wasn't doing much to help the cause along. The battle, Mackenzie knew, was up to him and Smith.

He wondered abstractedly where Nellie was.

"Probably halfway back to the post by now," he told himself, drawing a bead on the point from which came the most devastating blaze of firing.

But even as he depressed the firing button, the firing from below broke off in a chorus of sudden screams. The two Groombridgians leaped up and started to run, but before they made their second stride, something came whizzing through the air from the slope below and crumpled one of them.

The other hesitated, like a startled hare, uncertain where

to go, and a second thing came whishing up from the bottom of the slope and smacked against his breastplate with a thud that could be heard from where Mackenzie lay.

Then, for the first time Mackenzie saw Nellie. She was striding up the hill, her left arm holding an armful of stones hugged tight against her metal chest, her right arm working like a piston. The ringing clang of stone against metal came as one of the stones missed its mark and struck the ground car.

The human was running wildly, twisting and ducking, while Nellie pegged rock after rock at him. Trying to get set for a shot at her, the barrage of whizzing stones kept him on the dodge. Angling down the hill, he finally lost his rifle when he tripped and fell. With a howl of terror, he bolted up the hillside, his life blanket standing out almost straight behind him. Nellie pegged her last stone at him, then set out, doggedly loping in his wake.

Mackenzie screamed hoarsely at her, but she did not stop. She passed out of sight over the hill, closely behind the fleeing man.

Smith whooped with delight. "Look at our Nellie go for him," he yelled. "She'll give him a working over when she nails him."

Mackenzie rubbed his eyes. "Who was he?" he asked.

"Jack Alexander," said Smith. "Grant said he was around again."

The third man got up stiffly from behind his boulder and advanced toward them. He wore no life blanket, his clothing was in tatters, his face was bearded to the eyes.

He jerked a thumb toward the hill over which Nellie had disappeared. "A masterly military maneuver," he declared. "Your robot sneaked around and took them from behind."

"If she lost the recording stuff and the fertilizer, I'll melt her down," said Mackenzie, savagely.

The man stared at them. "You are the gentlemen from the trading post?" he asked.

They nodded, returning his stare.

"I am Wade," he said. "J. Edgerton Wade—"

"Wait a second," shouted Smith. "Not *the* J. Edgerton Wade? The lost composer?"

The man bowed, whiskers and all. "The same," he said. "Although I had not been aware that I was lost. I merely came out here to spend a year, a year of music such as man has never heard before."

He glared at them. "I am a man of peace," he declared, almost as if daring them to argue that he wasn't, "but when those three dug up Delbert, I knew what I must do."

"Delbert?" asked Mackenzie.

"The tree," said Wade. "One of the music trees."

"Those lousy planet-runners," said Smith, "figured they'd take that tree and sell it to someone back on Earth. I can think of a lot of big shots who'd pay plenty to have one of those trees in their back yard."

"It's a lucky thing we came along," said Mackenzie, soberly. "If we hadn't, if they'd got away with it, the whole planet would have gone on the warpath. We could have closed up shop. It might have been years before we dared come back again."

Smith rubbed his hands together, smirking. "We'll take back their precious tree," he declared, "and will that put us in solid! They'll give us their tunes from now on, free for nothing, just out of pure gratitude."

"You gentlemen," said Wade, "are motivated by mercenary factors but you have the right idea."

A heavy tread sounded behind them and when they turned they saw Nellie striding down the hill. She clutched a life blanket in her hand.

"He got away," she said, "but I got his blanket. Now I got a blanket, too, just like you fellows."

"What do you need with a life blanket?" yelled Smith. "You give that blanket to Mr. Wade. Right away. You hear me."

Nellie pouted. "You won't let me have anyting. You never act like I'm human—"

"You aren't," said Smith.

"If you give that blanket to Mr. Wade," wheedled Mackenzie, "I'll let you drive the car."

"You would?" asked Nellie, eagerly.

"Really," said Wade, shifting from one foot to the other, embarrassed.

"You take that blanket," said Mackenzie. "You need it. Looks like you haven't eaten for a day or two."

"I haven't," Wade confessed.

"Shuck into it then and get yourself a meal," said Smith.

Nellie handed it over.

"How come you were so good pegging those rocks?" asked Smith.

Nellie's eyes gleamed with pride. "Back on Earth I was on a baseball team," she said. "I was the pitcher."

Alexander's car was undamaged except for a few dents and a smashed vision plate where Wade's first bolt had caught it, blasting the glass and startling the operator so that he swerved sharply, spinning the treads across a boulder and upsetting it.

The music tree was unharmed, its roots still well

moistened in the burlap-wrapped, water-soaked ball of earth. Inside the tractor, curled in a tight ball in the darkest corner, unperturbed by the uproar that had been going on outside, they found Delbert, the two-foot high, roly-poly conductor that resembled nothing more than a poodle dog walking on its hind legs.

The Groombridgians were dead, their crushed chitinous armor proving the steam behind Nellie's delivery.

Smith and Wade were inside the tractor, settled down for the night. Nellie and the Encyclopedia were out in the night, hunting for the gun Alexander had dropped when he fled. Mackenzie, sitting on the ground, Nicodemus pulled snugly about him, leaned back against the car and smoked a last pipe before turning in.

The grass behind the tractor rustled.

"That you, Nellie?" Mackenzie called, softly.

Nellie clumped hesitantly around the corner of the car.

"You ain't sore at me?" she asked.

"No, I'm not sore at you. You can't help the way you are."

"I didn't find the gun," said Nellie.

"You knew where Alexander dropped it?"

"Yes," said Nellie. "It wasn't there."

Mackenzie frowned in the darkness. "That means Alexander managed to come back and get it. I don't like that. He'll be out gunning for us. He didn't like the company before. He'll really be out for blood after what we did today."

He looked around. "Where's the Encyclopedia?"

"I sneaked away from him. I wanted to talk to you about him."

"O.K.," said Mackenzie. "Fire away."

"He's been trying to read my brain," said Nellie.

"I know. He read the rest of ours. Did a good job of it."

"He's been having trouble," declared Nellie.

"Trouble reading your brain? I wouldn't doubt it."

"You don't need to talk as if my brain—" Nellie began, but Mackenzie stopped her.

"I don't mean it that way, Nellie. Your brain is all right, far as I know. Maybe even better than ours. But the point is that it's different. Ours are natural brains, the orthodox way for things to think and reason and remember. The Encyclopedia knows about those kinds of brains and the minds that go with them. Yours isn't that kind. It's artificial. Part mechanical, part chemical, part electrical, Lord knows what else; I'm not a robot technician. He's never run up against that kind of brain before. It probably has him down. Matter of fact, our civilization probably has him down. If this planet ever had a real civilization, it wasn't a mechanical one. There's no sign of mechanization here. None of the scars machines inflict on planets."

"I been fooling him," said Nellie quietly. "He's been trying to read my mind, but I been reading his."

Mackenzie started forward. "Well, I'll be—" he began. Then he settled back against the car, dead pipe hanging from between his teeth. "Why didn't you ever let us know you could read minds?" he demanded. "I suppose you been sneaking around all this time, reading our minds, making fun of us, laughing behind our backs."

"Honest, I ain't," said Nellie. "Cross my heart, I ain't. I didn't even know I could. But, when I felt the Encyclopedia prying around inside my head the way he does, it kind of got my dander up. I almost hauled off and smacked him one. And then I figured maybe I better be more subtle. I figured that if he could pry around in my mind, I could pry around in his. I tried it and it worked."

"Just like that," said Mackenzie.

"It wasn't hard," said Nellie. "It come natural. I seemed to just know how to do it."

"If the guy that made you knew what he'd let slip through his fingers, he'd cut his throat," Mackenzie told her.

Nellie sidled closer. "It scares me," she said.

"What's scaring you now?"

"That Encyclopedia knows too much."

"Alien stuff," said Mackenzie. "You should have expected that. Don't go messing around with an alien mentality unless you're ready for some shocks."

"It ain't that," said Nellie. "I knew I'd find alien stuff. But he knows other things. Things he shouldn't know."

"About us?"

"No, about other places. Places other than the Earth and this planet here. Places Earthmen ain't been to yet. The kind of things no Earthman could know by himself or that no Encyclopedia could know by himself, either."

"Like what?"

"Like knowing mathematical equations that don't sound like anything we know about," said Nellie. "Nor like he'd know about if he'd stayed here all his life. Equations you couldn't know unless you knew a lot more about space and time than even Earthmen know."

"Philosophy, too. Ideas that make sense in a funny sort of way, but make your head swim when you try to figure out the kind of people that would develop them."

Mackenzie got out his pouch and refilled his pipe, got it going.

"Nellie, you think maybe this Encyclopedia has been at other minds? Minds of other people who may have come here?"

"Could be," agreed Nellie. "Maybe a long time ago. He's awful old. Lets on he could be immortal if he wanted to be. Said he wouldn't die until there was nothing more in the universe to know. Said when the time came there'd be nothing more to live for."

Mackenzie clicked his pipestem against his teeth. "He could be, too," he said. "Immortal, I mean. Plants haven't got all the physiological complications animals have. Given any sort of care, they theoretically could live forever."

Grass rustled on the hillside above them and Mackenzie settled back against the car, kept on smoking. Nellie hunkered down a few feet away.

The Encyclopedia waddled down the hill, starlight glinting from his shell-like back. Ponderously he lined up with them beside the car, pushing his taproot into the ground for an evening snack.

"Understand you may be going back to Earth with us," said Mackenzie, conversationally.

The answer came, measured in sharp and concise thought that seemed to drill deep into Mackenzie's mind. "I should like to. Your race is interesting."

It was hard to talk to a thing like that, Mackenzie told himself. Hard to keep the chatter casual when you knew all the time it was hunting around in the corners of your mind. Hard to match one's voice against the brittle thought with which it talked.

"What do you think of us?" he asked and knew, as soon as he had asked it, that it was asinine.

"I know very little of you," the Encyclopedia declared. "You have created artificial lives, while we on this planet have lived natural lives. You have bent every force that you can master to your will. You have made things work for you. First impression is that, potentially, you are dangerous."

"I guess I asked for it," Mackenzie said.

"I do not follow you."

"Skip it," said Mackenzie.

"The only trouble," said the Encyclopedia, "is that you don't know where you're going."

"That's what makes it so much fun," Mackenzie told him. "Cripes, if we knew where we were going there'd be no adventure. We'd know what was coming next. As it is, every corner that we turn brings a new surprise."

"Knowing where you're going has its advantages," insisted the Encyclopedia.

Mackenzie knocked the pipe bowl out on his boot heel, tramped on the glowing ash.

"So you have us pegged," he said.

"No," said the Encyclopedia. "Just first impressions."

The music trees were twisted gray ghosts in the murky dawn. The conductors, except for the few who refused to let even a visit from the Earthmen rouse them from their daylight slumber, squatted like black imps on their podia.

Delbert rode on Smith's shoulder, one clawlike hand entwined in Smith's hair to keep from falling off. The Encyclopedia waddled along in the wake of the Earthman party. Wade led the way toward Alder's podium.

Thc Bowl buzzed with the hum of distorted thought, the thought of many little folk squatting on their mounds—an alien thing that made Mackenzie's neck hairs bristle just a little as it beat into his mind. There were no really separate thoughts, no one commanding thought, just the chitter-chatter of hundreds of little thoughts, as if the conductors might be gossiping.

The yellow cliffs stood like a sentinel wall and above the path that led to the escarpment, the tractor loomed like a straddled beetle against the early dawn.

Alder rose from the podium to greet them, a disreptuable-looking gnome on gnarly legs.

The Earth delegation squatted on the ground. Delbert, from his perch on Smith's shoulder, made a face at Adler.

Silence held for a moment and then Mackenzie, dispensing with formalities, spoke to Adler. "We rescued Delbert for you," he told the gnome. "We brought him back."

Alder scowled and his thoughts were fuzzy with disgust. "We do not want him back," he said.

Mackenzie taken aback, stammered. "Why, we thought... that is, he's one of you... we went to a lot of trouble to rescue him—"

"He's a nuisance," declared Alder. "He's a disgrace. He's a no-good. He's always trying things."

"You're not so hot yourself," piped Delbert's thought. "Just a bunch of fuddy-duddies. A crowd of corn peddlers. You're sore at me because I want to be different. Because I dust it off—"

"You see," said Alder to Mackenzie, "what he is like."

"Why, yes," agreed Mackenzie, "but there are times when new ideas have some values. Perhaps he may be—"

Alder leveled an accusing finger at Wade. "He was all right until you took to hanging around," he screamed. "Then he picked up some of your ideas. You contaminated him. Your silly notions about music—" Alder's thoughts gulped in sheer exasperation, then took up again. "Why did you come? No one asked you to? Why don't you mind your own business?"

Wade, red faced behind his beard, seemed close to apoplexy.

"I've never been so insulted in all my life," he howled. He thumped his chest with a doubled fist. "Back on Earth I wrote great symphonies myself. I never held with frivolous music. I never—"

"Crawl back into your hole," Delbert shrilled at Alder. "You guys don't know what music is. You saw out the same stuff day after day. You never lay it in the groove. You never get gated up. You all got long underwear."

Alder waved knotted fists above his head and hopped up and down in rage. "Such language!" he shrieked. "Never was the like heard here before."

The whole Bowl was yammering. Yammering with clashing thoughts of rage and insult.

"Wait," Mackenzie shouted. "All of you, quiet down!"

Wade puffed out his breath, turned a shade less purple. Alder squatted back on his haunches, unknotted his fists, tried his best to look composed. The clamor of thought subsided to a murmur.

"You're sure about this?" Mackenzie asked Alder. "Sure you don't want Delbert back."

"Mister," said Alder, "there never was a happier day in Melody Bowl than the day we found him gone."

A rising murmur of assent from the other conductors underscored his words.

"Wc have some others we'd like to get rid of, too," said Alder.

From far across the Bowl came a yelping thought of derision.

"You see," said Alder, looking owlishly at Mackenzie, "what it is like. What we have to contend with. All because this . . . this . . . this—"

Glaring at Wade, thoughts failed him. Carefully he settled back upon his haunches, composed his face again.

"If the rest were gone," he said, "we could settle down. But as it is, these few keep us in an uproar all the time. We can't concentrate, we can't really work. We can't do the things we want to do."

Mackenzie pushed back his hat and scratched his head.

"Alder, he declared, "you sure are in a mess."

"I was hoping," Alder said, "that you might be able to take them off our hands."

"Take them off your hands!" yelled Smith. "I'll say we'll take them! We'll take as many—"

Mackenzie nudged Smith in the ribs with his elbow, viciously. Smith gulped into silence. Mackenzie tried to keep his face straight.

"You can't take them trees," said Nellie, icily. "It's against the law."

Mackenzie gasped. "The law?"

"Sure, the regulations. The company's got regulations. Or don't you know that? Never bothered to read them, probably. Just like you. Never pay no attention to the things you should."

"Nellie," said Smith savagely, "you keep out of this. I guess if we want to do a little favor for Alder here—"

"But it's against the law!" screeched Nellie.

"I know," said Mackenzie. "Section 34 of the chapter on Relations with Extraterrestrial Life. *'No member of this company shall interfere in any phase of the internal affairs of another race.'* "

"That's it," said Nellie, pleased with herself. "And if you take some of these trees, you'll be meddling in a quarrel that you have no business having anything to do with."

Mackenzie flipped his hands. "You see," he said to Alder.

"We'll give you a monopoly on our music," tempted Alder. "We'll let you know when we have anything. We won't let the Groomies have it and we'll keep our prices right."

Nellie shook her head. "No," she said.

Alder bargained. "Bushel and a half instead of two bushel."

"No," said Nellie.

"It's a deal," declared Mackenzie. "Just point out your duds and we'll haul them away."

"But Nellie said no," Alder pointed out. "And you say yes. I don't understand."

"We'll take care of Nellie," Smith told him, soberly.

"You won't take them trees," said Nellie. "I won't let you take them. I'll see to that."

"Don't pay any attention to her," Mackenzie said. "Just point out the ones you want to get rid of."

Alder said primly: "You've made us very happy."

Mackenzie got up and looked around. "Where's the Encyclopedia?" he asked.

"He cleared out a minute ago," said Smith. "Headed back for the car."

Mackenzie saw him, scuttling swiftly up the path toward the cliff top.

It was topsy-turvy and utterly crazy, like something out of that old book for children written by a man named Carroll. There was no sense to it. It was like taking candy from a baby.

Walking up the cliff path back to the tractor, Mackenzie knew it was, felt that he should pinch himself to know it was no dream.

He had hoped—just hoped—to avert relentless, merciless war against Earthmen throughout the planet by bringing back the stolen music tree. And here he was, with other music trees for his own, and a bargain thrown in to boot.

There was something wrong, Mackenzie told himself, something utterly and nonsensically wrong. But he couldn't put his finger on it.

There was no need to worry, he told himself. The thing to do was to get those trees and get out of there before Alder and the others changed their minds.

"It's funny," Wade said behind him.

"It is," agreed Mackenzie. "Everything is funny here."

"I mean about those trees," said Wade. "I'd swear Delbert was all right. So were all the others. They played the same music the others played. If there had been any faulty orchestration, any digression from form, I am sure I would have noticed it."

Mackenzie spun around and grasped Wade by the arm. "You mean they weren't lousing up the concerts? That Delbert, here, played just like the rest?"

Wade nodded.

"That ain't so," shrilled Delbert from his perch on Smith's shoulder. "I wouldn't play like the rest of them. I want to kick the stuff around. I always dig it up and hang it out the window. I dream it up and send it away out wide."

"Where'd you pick up that lingo?" Mackenzie snapped. "I never heard anything like it before."

"I learned it from him," declared Delbert, pointing at Wade.

Wade's face was purple and his eyes were glassy.

"It's practically prehistoric," he gulped. "It's terms that were used back in the twentieth century to describe a certain kind of popular rendition. I read about it in a history covering the origins of music. There was a glossary of terms. They were so fantastic they stuck in my mind."

Smith puckered his lips, whistling soundlessly. "So that's how he picked it up. He caught it from your thoughts. Same principle that Encyclopedia uses, although not so advanced."

"He lacks the Encyclopedia's distinction," explained Mackenzie. "He didn't know the stuff he was picking up was something that had happened long ago."

"I have a notion to wring his neck," Wade threatened.

"You'll keep your hands off him," grated Mackenzie. "This deal stinks to the high heavens, but seven music trees are seven music trees. Screwy deal or not, I'm going through with it."

"Look fellows," said Nellie, "I wish you wouldn't do it."

Mackenzie puckered his brow. "What's the matter with you, Nellie? Why did you make that uproar about the law down there? There's a rule, sure, but in a thing like this it's different. The company can afford to have a rule or two broken for seven music trees. You know what will happen, don't you, when we get those trees back home. We can charge a thousand bucks a throw to hear them and have to use a club to keep the crowds away."

"And the best of it is," Smith pointed out, "that once they hear them, they'll have to come again. They'll never get tired of them. Instead of that, every time they hear them, they'll want to hear them all the more. It'll get to be an obsession, a part of the people's life. They'll steal, murder, do anything so they can hear the trees."

"That," said Mackenzie, soberly, "is the one thing I'm afraid of."

"I only tried to stop you," Nellie said. "I know as well as you do that the law won't hold in a thing like this. But there was something else. The way the conductors sounded. Almost as if they were jeering at us. Like a gang of boys out in the street hooting at someone they just pulled a fast one on."

"You're batty," Smith declared.

"We have to go through with it," Mackenzie announced, flatly. "If anyone ever found we'd let a chance like this slip through our fingers, they'd crucify us for it."

"You're going to get in touch with Harper?" Smith asked.

Mackenzie nodded. "We have to get hold of Earth, have them send out a ship right away to take back the trees."

"I still think," said Nellie, "there's a nigger in the woodpile."

• • •

Mackenzie flipped the toggle and the visiphone went dead.

Harper had been hard to convince. Mackenzie, thinking about it, couldn't blame him much. After all, it did sound incredible. But then, this whole planet was incredible.

Mackenzie reached into his pocket and hauled forth his pipe and pouch. Nellie probably would raise hell about helping to dig up those other six trees, but she'd have to get over it. They'd have to work as fast as they could. They couldn't spend more than one night up here on the rim. There wasn't enough serum for longer than that. One jug of the stuff wouldn't go too far.

Suddenly excited shouts came from outside the car, shouts of consternation.

With a single leap, Mackenzie left the chair and jumped for the door. Outside, he almost bumped into Smith, who came running around the corner of the tractor. Wade, who had been down at the cliff's edge, was racing toward them.

"It's Nellie," shouted Smith. "Look at that robot!"

Nellie was marching toward them, dragging in her wake a thing that bounced and struggled. A rifle-tree grove fired a volley and one of the pellets caught Nellie in the shoulder, puffing into dust, staggering her a little.

The bouncing thing was the Encyclopedia. Nellie had hold of his taproot, was hauling him unceremoniously across the bumpy ground.

"Put him down!" Mackenzie yelled at her. "Let him go!"

"He stole the serum," howled Nellie. "He stole the serum and broke it on a rock!"

She swung the Encyclopedia toward them in a looping

heave. The intelligent vegetable bounced a couple of times, struggled to get right side up, then scurried off a few feet, root coiled tightly against its underside.

Smith moved toward it threateningly. "I ought to kick the living innards out of you," he yelled. "We need that serum. You knew why we needed it."

"You threaten me with force," said the Encyclopedia. "The most primitive method of compulsion."

"It works," Smith told him shortly.

The Encyclopedia's thoughts were unruffled, almost serene, as clear and concise as ever. "You have a law that forbids your threatening or harming any alien thing."

"Chum," declared Smith, "you better get wised up on laws. There are times when certain laws don't hold. And this is one of them."

"Just a minute," said Mackenzie. He spoke to the Encyclopedia. "What is your understanding of a law?"

"It is a rule you live by," the Encyclopedia said. "It is-something that is necessary. You cannot violate it."

"He got that from Nellie," said Smith.

"You think because there is a law against it, we won't take the trees?"

"There is a law against it," said the Encyclopedia. "You cannot take the trees."

"So as soon as you found that out, you lammed up here and stole the serum, eh!"

"He's figuring on indoctrinating us," Nellie explained. "Maybe that word ain't so good. Maybe conditioning is better. It's sort of mixed up. I don't know if I've got it straight. He took the serum so we would hear the trees without being able to defend ourselves against them. He figured when we heard the music, we'd go ahead and take the trees."

"Law or no law?"

"That's it," Nellie said. "Law or no law."

Smith whirled on the robot. "What kind of jabber is this? How do you know what he was planning?"

"I read his mind," said Nellie. "Hard to get at, the thing that he was planning, because he kept it deep. But some of it jarred up where I could reach it when you threatened him."

"You can't do that!" shrieked the Encyclopedia. "Not you! Not a machine!"

Mackenzie laughed shortly. "Too bad, big boy, but she can. She's been doing it."

Smith stared at Mackenzie.

"It's all right," Mackenzie said. "It isn't any bluff. She told me about it last night."

"You are unduly alarmed," the Encyclopedia said. "You are putting a wrong interpretation—"

A quiet voice spoke, almost as if it were a voice inside Mackenzie's mind.

"Don't believe a thing he tells you, pal. Don't fall for any of his lies."

"Nicodemus! You know something about this?"

"It's the trees," said Nicodemus. "The music does something to you. It changes you. Makes you different than you were before. Wade is different. He doesn't know it, but he is."

"If you mean the music chains one to it, that is true," said Wade. "I may as well admit it. I could not live without the music. I could not leave the Bowl. Perhaps you gentlemen thought that I would go back with you. But I cannot go. I cannot leave. It will work the same with anyone. Alexander was here for a while when he ran short of serum. Doctors treated him and he was all right, but he came back. He had to come back. He couldn't stay away."

"It isn't only that," declared Nicodemus. "It changes you, too, in other ways. It can change you any way it wants to. Change your way of thinking. Change your viewpoints."

Wade strode forward. "It isn't true," he yelled. "I'm the same as when I came here."

"You heard things," said Nicodemus, "felt things in the music you couldn't understand. Things you wanted to understand, but couldn't. Strange emotions that you yearned to share, but could never reach. Strange thoughts that tantalized you for days."

Wade sobered, stared at them with haunted eyes.

"That was the way it was," he whispered. "That was just the way it was."

He glanced around, like a trapped animal seeking escape.

"But I don't feel any different," he mumbled. "I still am human. I think like a man, act like a man.-'

"Of course you do," said Nicodemus. "Otherwise you would have been scared away. If you had known what was happening to you, you wouldn't let it happen. And you have had less than a year of it. Less than a year of this conditioning. Five years and you would be less human. Ten years and you would be beginning to be the kind of thing the trees want you to be."

"And we were going to take some of those trees to Earth!" Smith shouted. "Seven of them! So the people of the Earth could hear them. Listen to them, night after night. The whole world listening to them on the radio. A whole world being conditioned, being changed by seven music trees."

"But why?" asked Wade, bewildered.

"Why did men domesticate animals?" Mackenzie asked. "You wouldn't find out by asking the animals, for they don't know. There is just as much point asking a dog why he was domesticated as there is in asking us why the trees want to condition us. For some purpose of their own, undoubtedly, that is perfectly clear and logical to them. A purpose that undoubtedly never can be clear and logical to us."

"Nicodemus," said the Encyclopedia and his thought was deathly cold, "you have betrayed your own."

Mackenzie laughed harshly. "You're wrong there," he told the vegetable, "because Nicodemus isn't a plant, any more. He's a human. The same thing has happened to him as you want to have happen to us. He has become a human in everything but physical make-up. He thinks as a man does. His viewpoints are ours, not yours."

"That is right," said Nicodemus. "I am a man."

A piece of cloth ripped savagely and for an instant the group was blinded by a surge of energy that leaped from the thicket a hundred yards away. Smith gurgled once in sudden agony and the energy was gone.

Frozen momentarily by surprise, Mackenzie watched Smith stagger, face tight with pain, hand clapped to his side. Slowly the man wilted, sagged in the middle and went down.

Silently, Nellie leaped forward, was sprinting for the thicket. With a hoarse cry, Mackenzie bent over Smith.

Smith grinned at him, a twisted grin. His mouth worked, but no words came. His hand slid away from his side and he went limp, but his chest rose and fell with a slightly slower breath. His life blanket had shifted its position to cover the wounded side.

Mackenzie straightened up, hauling the pistol from his

belt. A man had risen from the thicket, was leveling a gun at the charging Nellie. With a wild yell, Mackenzie shot from the hip. The lashing charge missed the man but half the thicket disappeared in a blinding sheet of flame.

The man with the gun ducked as the flame puffed out at him and in that instant Nellie closed in. The man yelled once,

a long-drawn howl of terror as Nellie swung him above her head and dashed him down. The smoking thicket hid the rest of it. Mackenzie, pistol hanging limply by his side, watched Nellie's right fist lift and fall with brutal precision, heard the thud of life being beaten from a human body.

Sickened, he turned back to Smith. Wade was kneeling beside the wounded man. He looked up.

"He seems to be unconscious."

Mackenzie nodded. "The blanket put him out. Gave him an anaesthesia. It'll take care of him."

Mackenzie glanced up sharply at a scurry in the grass. The Encyclopedia, taking advantage of the moment, was almost out of sight, scuttling toward a grove of rifle trees.

A step grated behind him.

"It was Alexander," Nellie said. "He won't bother us no more."

Nelson Harper, factor at the post, was lighting up his pipe when the visiphone signal buzzed and the light flashed on.

Startled, Harper reached out and snapped on the set. Mackenzie's face came in, a face streaked with dirt and perspiration, stark with fear. He waited for no greeting. His lips were already moving even as the plate flickered and cleared.

"It's all off, chief," he said. "The deal is off. I can't bring in those trees."

"You got to bring them in," yelled Harper. "I've already called Earth. I got them turning handsprings. They say it's the greatest thing that ever happened. They're sending out a ship within an hour."

"Call them back and tell them not to bother," Mackenzie snapped.

"But you told me everything was set," yelped Harper. "You told me nothing could happen. You said you'd bring them in if you had to crawl on hands and knees and pack them on your back."

"I told you every word of that," agreed Mackenzie. "Probably even more. But I didn't know what I know now."

Harper groaned. "Galactic is plastering every front page in the Solar System with the news. Earth radios right now are bellowing it out from Mercury to Pluto. Before another hour is gone every man, woman and child will know those trees are coming to Earth. And once they know that, there's nothing we can do. Do you understand that, Mackenzie? We have to get them there!"

"I can't do it, chief," Mackenzie insisted, stubbornly.

"Why can't you?" screamed Harper. "So help me Hannah, if you don't—"

"I can't bring them in because Nellie's burning them. She's down in the Bowl right now with a flamer. When she's through, there won't be any music trees."

"Go out and stop her!" shrieked Harper. "What are you sitting there for! Go out and stop her! Blast her if you have to. Do anything, but stop her! That crazy robot—"

"I told her to," snapped Mackenzie. "I ordered her to do it. When I get through here, I'm going down to help her."

"You're crazy, man!" yelled Harper. "Stark, staring crazy. They'll throw the book at you for this. You'll be lucky if you just get life—"

Two darting hands loomed in the plate, hands that snapped down and closed around Mackenzie's throat, hands that dragged him away and left the screen blank, but with a certain blurring motion, as if two men might be fighting for their lives just in front of it.

"Mackenzie!" screamed Harper. "Mackenzie!"

Something smashed into the screen and shattered it, leaving the broken glass gaping in jaggged shards.

Harper clawed at the visiphone. "Mackenzie! Mackenzie, what's happening!"

In answer the screen exploded in a flash of violent flame, howled like a screeching banshee and then went dead.

Harper stood frozen in the room, listening to the faint purring of the radio. His pipe fell from his hand and bounced along the floor spilling burned tobacco.

Cold, clammy fear closed down upon him, squeezing his heart. A fear that twisted him and mocked him. Galactic would break him for this, he knew. Send him out to some of the jungle planets as the rankest subordinate. He would be marked for life, a man not to be trusted, a man who had failed to uphold the prestige of the company.

Suddenly a faint spark of hope stirred deep within him. If he could get there soon enough! If he could get to Melody Bowl in time, he might stop this madness. Might at least save something, save a few of the precious trees.

The flier was in the compound, waiting. Within half an hour he could be above the Bowl.

He leaped for the door, shoved it open and even as he did a pellet whistled past his cheek and exploded into a puff of dust against the door frame. Instinctively, he ducked and another pellet brushed his hair. A third caught him in the leg with stinging force and brought him down. A fourth puffed dust into his face.

He fought his way to his knees, was staggered by another shot that slammed into his side. He raised his right arm to protect his face and a sledge-hammer blow slapped his wrist. Pain flowed along his arm and in sheer panic he turned and scrambled on hands and knees across the threshold and kicked the door shut with his foot.

Sitting flat on the floor, he held his right wrist in his left hand. He tried to make his fingers wiggle and they wouldn't. The wrist, he knew, was broken.

After weeks of being off the beam, the rifle tree outside the compound suddenly had regained its aim and gone on a rampage.

Mackenzie raised himself off the floor and braced himself with one elbow, while with the other hand he fumbled at his throbbing throat. The interior of the tractor danced with wavy motion and his head thumped and pounded with pain.

Slowly, carefully, he inched himself back so he could lean against the wall. Gradually the room stopped rocking, but the pounding in his head went on.

Someone was standing in the doorway of the tractor and he fought to focus his eyes, trying to make out who it was.

A voice screeched across his nerves.

"I'm taking your blankets. You'll get them back when you decide to leave the trees alone."

Mackenzie tried to fashion words, but all he accomplished was a croak. He tried again.

"Wade?" he asked.

It was Wade, he saw.

The man stood within the doorway, one hand clutching a pair of blankets, the other holding a gun.

"You're crazy, Wade," he whispered. "We have to burn the trees. The human race never would be safe. Even if they fail this time, they'll try again. And again—and yet again. And some day they will get us. Even without going to Earth they can get us. They can twist us to their purpose with recordings alone: Long distance propaganda. Take a bit longer, but it will do the job as well."

"They are beautiful," said Wade. "The most beautiful things in all the universe. I can't let you destroy them. You must not destroy them."

"But can't you see," croaked Mackenzie, "that's the thing that makes them so dangerous. Their beauty, the beauty of their music, is fatal. No one can resist it."

"It was the thing I lived by," Wade told him, soberly. "You say it made me something that was not quite human. But what difference does that make. Must racial purity, in thought and action, be a fetish that would chain us to a drab existence when something better, something greater, is offered. And we never would have known. That is the best of it all, we never would have known. They would have changed us, yes, but so slowly, so gradually, that we would not have suspected. Our decisions and our actions and our way of thought would still have seemed to be our own. The trees never would have been anything more than something cultural."

"They want our mechanization," said Mackenzie. "Plants can't develop machines. Given that, they might have taken us along a road we, in our rightful heritage, never would have taken."

"How can we be sure," asked Wade, "that our heritage would have guided us aright?"

Mackenzie slid straighter against the wall. His head still throbbed and his throat still ached.

"You've been thinking about this?" he asked.

Wade nodded. "At first there was the natural reaction of horror. But, logically, that reaction is erroneous. Our schools teach our children a way of life. Our press strives to formulate our adult opinion and belief. The trees were doing no more to us than we do to ourselves. And perhaps, for a purpose no more selfish."

Mackenzie shook his head. "We must live our own life. We must follow the path the attributes of humanity decree that we should follow. And anyway, you're wasting your time."

"I don't understand," said Wade.

"Nellie already is burning the trees," Mackenzie told him. "I sent her out before I made the call to Harper."

"No, she's not," said Wade.

Mackenzie sat bolt upright. "What do you mean?"

Wade flipped the pistol as Mackenzie moved as if to regain his feet.

"It doesn't matter what I mean," he snapped. "Nellie isn't burning any trees. She isn't in a position to burn any trees. And neither are you, for I've taken both your flamers. And the tractor won't run, either. I've seen to that. So the only thing that you can do is stay right here."

Mackenzie motioned toward Smith, lying on the floor. "You're taking his blanket, too?"

Wade nodded.

"But you can't. Smith will die. Without that blanket he doesn't have a chance. The blanket could have healed the wound, kept him fed correctly, kept him warm—"

"That," said Wade, "is all the more reason that you come to terms directly."

"Your terms," said Mackenzie, "are that we leave the trees unharmed.

"Those are my terms."

Mackenzie shook his head. "I can't take the chance," he said.

"When you decide, just step out and shout," Wade told him. "I'll stay in calling distance."

He backed slowly from the door.

Smith needed warmth and food. In the hour since his blanket had been taken from him he had regained consciousness, had mumbled feverishly and tossed about, his hand clawing at his wounded side.

Squatting beside him, Mackenzie had tried to quiet him, had felt a wave of slow terror as he thought of the hours ahead.

There was no food in the tractor, no means for making heat. There was no need for such provision so long as they had had their life blankets—but now the blankets were gone. There was a first-aid cabinet and with the materials that he found there, Mackenzie did his fumbling best, but there was nothing to relieve Smith's pain, nothing to control his fever. For treatment such as that they had relied upon the blankets.

The atomic motor might have been rigged up to furnish heat, but Wade had taken the firing mechanism control.

Night was falling and that meant the air would grow colder. Not too cold to live, of course, but cold enough to spell doom to a man in Smith's condition.

Mackenzie squatted on his heels and stared at Smith.

"If I could only find Nellie," he thought.

He had tried to find her—briefly. He had raced along the rim of the Bowl for a mile or so, but had seen no sign of her. He had been afraid to go farther, afraid to stay too long from the man back in the tractor.

Smith mumbled and Mackenzie bent low to try to catch the words. But there were no words.

Slowly he rose and headed for the door. First of all, he needed heat. Then food. The heat came first. An open fire wasn't the best way to make heat, of course, but it was better than nothing.

The uprooted music tree, balled roots silhouetted against the sky, loomed before him in the dusk. He found a few dead branches and tore them off. They would do to start the fire. After that he would have to rely on green wood to keep it going. Tomorrow he could forage about for suitable fuel.

In the Bowl below, the music trees were tuning up for the evening concert.

Back in the tractor, he found a knife, carefully slivered several of the branches for easy lighting, piled them ready for his pocket lighter.

The lighter flared and a tiny figure hopped up on the threshold of the tractor, squatting there, blinking at the light.

Startled, Mackenzie held the lighter without touching it to the wood, stared at the thing that perched in the doorway.

Delbert's squeaky thought drilled into his brain.

"What you doing?"

"Building a fire," Mackenzie told him.

"What's a fire?"

"It's a . . . it's a . . . say, don't you know what a fire is?"

"Nope," said Delbert.

"It's a chemical action," Mackenzie said. "It breaks up matter and releases energy in the form of heat."

"What you building a fire with?" asked Delbert, blinking in the flare of the lighter.

"With branches from a tree."

Delbert's eyes widened and his thought was jittery.

"A tree?"

"Sure, a tree. Wood. It burns. It gives off heat. I need heat."

"What tree?"

"Why—" And then Mackenzie stopped with sudden realization. His thumb relaxed and the flame went out.

Delbert shrieked at him in sudden terror and anger. "It's my tree! You're building a fire with my tree!"

Mackenzie sat in silence.

"When you burn my tree, it's gone," yelled Delbert. "Isn't that right? When you burn my tree, it's gone?"

Mackenzie nodded.

"But why do you do it?" shrilled Delbert.

"I need heat," said Mackenzie, doggedly. "If I don't have heat, my friend will die. It's the only way I can get heat."

"But my tree!"

Mackenzie shrugged. "I need a fire, see? And I'm getting it any way I can."

He flipped his thumb again and the lighter flared.

"But I never did anything to you," Delbert howled, rocking on the metal door sill. "I'm your friend, I am. I never did a thing to hurt you."

"No?" asked Mackenzie.

"No," yelled Delbert.

"What about that scheme of yours?" asked Mackenzie. "Trying to trick me into taking trees to Earth?"

"That wasn't my idea," yipped Delbert. "It wasn't any of the trees' ideas. The Encyclopedia thought it up."

• • •

A bulky form loomed outside the door. "Someone talking about me?" it asked.

The Encyclopedia was back again.

Arrogantly, he shouldered Delbert aside, stepped into the tractor.

"I saw Wade," he said.

Mackenzie glared at him. "So you figured it would be safe to come."

"Certainly," said the Encyclopedia. "Your formula of force counts for nothing now. You have no means to enforce it."

Mackenzie's hand shot out and grasped the Encyclopedia with a vicious grip, hurled him into the interor of the tractor.

"Just try to get out this door," he snarled. "You'll soon find out if the formula of force amounts to anything."

The Encyclopedia picked himself up, shook himself like a ruffled hen. But his thought was cool and calm.

"I can't see what this avails you."

"It gives us soup," Mackenzie snapped.

He sized the Encyclopedia up. "Good vegetable soup. Something like cabbage. Never cared much for cabbage soup, myself, but—"

"Soup?"

"Yeah, soup. Stuff to eat. Food."

"Food!" The Encyclopedia's thought held a tremor of anxiety. "You would use me as food."

"Why not?" Mackenzie asked him. "You're nothing but a vegetable. An intelligent vegetable, granted, but still a vegetable."

He felt the Encyclopedia's groping thought-fingers prying into his mind.

"Go ahead," he told him, "but you won't like what you find."

The Encyclopedia's thoughts almost gasped. "You withheld this from me!" he charged.

"We withheld nothing from you," Mackenzie declared. "We never had occasion to think of it . . . to remember to what use Men at one time put plants, to what use we still put plants in certain cases. The only reason we don't use them so extensively now is that we have advanced beyond the need of them. Let that need exist again and—"

"You ate us," strummed the Encyclopedia. "You used us to build your shelters! You destroyed us to create heat for your selfish purposes!"

"Pipe down," Mackenzie told him. "It's the way we did it that gets you. The idea that we thought we had a right to. That we went out and took, without even asking, never wondering what the plant might think about it. That hurts your racial dignity."

He stopped, then moved closer to the doorway. From the Bowl below came the first strains of the music. The tuning up, the preliminary to the concert was over.

"O.K.," Mackenzie said, "I'll hurt it some more. Even you are nothing but a plant to me. Just because you've learned some civilized tricks doesn't make you my equal. It never did. We humans can't slur off the experiences of the past so easily. It would take thousands of years of association with things like you before we even began to regard you as anything other than a plant, a thing that we used in the past and might use again."

"Still cabbage soup," said the Encyclopedia.

"Still cabbage soup," Mackenzie told him.

The music stopped. Stopped dead still, in the middle of a note.

"See," said Mackenzie, "even the music fails you."

Silence rolled at them in engulfing waves and through the stillness came another sound, the *clop, clop* of heavy, plodding feet.

"Nellie!" yelled Mackenzie.

A bulky shadow loomed in the darkness.

"Yeah, chief, it's me," said Nellie. "I brung you something."

She dumped Wade across the doorway.

Wade rolled over and groaned. There were skittering, flapping sounds as two fluttering shapes detached themselves from Wade's shoulders.

"Nellie," said Mackenzie, harshly, "there was no need to beat him up. You should have brought him back just as he was and let me take care of him."

"Gee, boss," protested Nellie. "I didn't beat him up. He was like that when I found him."

Nicodemus was clawing his way to Mackenzie's shoulder, while Smith's life blanket scuttled for the corner where his master lay.

"It was us, boss," piped Nicodemus. "We laid him out."

"You laid him out?"

"Sure, there was two of us and only one of him. We fed him poison."

Nicodemus settled into place on Mackenzie's shoulders.

"I didn't like him," he declared. "He wasn't nothing

like you, boss. I didn't want to change like him. I wanted to stay like you."

"This poison?" asked Mackenzie. "Nothing fatal, I hope."

"Sure not, pal," Nicodemus told him. "We only made him sick. He didn't know what was happening until it was too late to do anything about it. We bargained with him, we did. We told him we'd quit feeding it to him if he took us back. He was on his way here, too, but he'd never made it if it hadn't been for Nellie."

"Chief," pleaded Nellie, "when he gets so he knows what it's all about, won't you let me have him for about five minutes?"

"No," said Mackenzie.

"He strung me up," wailed Nellie. "He hid in the cliff and lassoed me and left me hanging there. It took me hours to get loose. Honest, I wouldn't hurt him much. I'd just kick him around a little, gentlelike."

From the cliff top came the rustling of grass as if hundreds of little feet were advancing upon them.

"We got visitors," said Nicodemus.

The visitors, Mackenzie saw, were the conductors, dozens of little gnomelike figures that moved up and squatted on their haunches, faintly luminous eyes blinking at them.

One of them shambled forward. As he came closer, Mackenzie saw that it was Alder.

"Well?" Mackenzie demanded.

"We came to tell you the deal is off," Alder squeaked. "Delbert came and told us."

"Told you what?"

"About what you do to trees."

"Oh, that."

"Yes, that."

"But you made the deal," Mackenzie told him. "You can't back out know. Why, Earth is waiting breathless—"

"Don't try to kid me," snapped Alder. "You don't want us any more than we want you. It was a dirty trick to start with, but it wasn't any of our doing. The Encyclopedia talked us into it. He told us we had a duty. A duty to our race. To act as missionaries to the inferior races of the Galaxy.

"We didn't take to it at first. Music, you see, is our life. We have been creating music for so long that our origin is lost in the dim antiquity of a planet that long ago has passed its zenith of existence. We will be creating music in that far day when the planet falls apart beneath our feet. You live by a code of accomplishment by action. We live by a code of accomplishment by music. Kadmar's Red Sun symphony was a greater triumph for us than the discovery of a new planetary system is for you. It pleased us when you liked our music. It will please us if you still like our music, even after what has happened. But we will not allow you to take any of us to Earth."

"The monopoly on the music still stands?" asked Mackenzie.

"It still stands. Come whenever you want to and record my symphony. When there are others we will let you know."

"And the propaganda in the music?"

"From now on," Alder promised, "the propaganda is out. If, from now on, our music changes you, it will change you through its own power. It may do that, but we will not try to shape your lives."

"How can we depend on that?"

"Certainly," said Alder. "There are certain tests you could devise. Not that they will be necessary."

"We'll devise the tests," declared Mackenzie. "Sorry, but we can't trust you."

"I'm sorry that you can't," said Alder, and he sounded as if he were.

"I was going to burn you," Mackenzie said, snapping his words off brutally. "Destroy you. Wipe you out. There was nothing you could have done about it. Nothing you could have done to stop me."

"You're still barbarians," Alder told him. "You have conquered the distances between the stars, you have built a great civilization, but your methods are still ruthless and degenerate."

"The Encyclopedia calls it a formula of force," Mackenzie said. "No matter what you call it, it still works. It's the thing that took us up. I warn you. If you ever again try to trick the human race, there will be hell to pay. A human being will destroy anything to save himself. Remember that—we destroy anything that threatens us."

Something swished out of the tractor door and Mackenzie whirled about.

"It's the Encyclopedia!" he yelled. "He's trying to get away! Nellie!"

There was a thrashing rustle. "Got him, boss," said Nellie.

The robot came out of the darkness, dragging the Encyclopedia along by his leafy topknot.

Mackenzie turned back to the composers, but the composers were gone. The grass rustled eerily toward the cliff edge as dozens of tiny feet scurried through it.

"What now?" asked Nellie. "Do we burn the trees?"

Mackenzie shook his head. "No, Nellie. We won't burn them."

"We got them scared," said Nellie. "Scared pink with purple spots."

"Perhaps we have," said Mackenzie. "Let's hope so, at least. But it isn't only that they're scared. They probably loathe us and that is better yet. Like we'd loathe some form of life that bred and reared men for food—that thought of Man as nothing else than food. All the time they've thought of themselves as the greatest intellectual force in the universe. We've given them a jolt. We've scared them and hurt their pride and shook their confidence. They've run up against something that is more than a match for them. Maybe they'll think twice again before they try any more shenanigans."

Down in the Bowl the music began again.

Mackenzie went in to look at Smith. The man was sleeping peacefully, his blanket wrapped around him. Wade sat in a corner, head held in his hands.

Outside, a rocket murmured and Nellie yelled. Mackenzie spun on his heel and dashed through the door. A ship was swinging over the Bowl, lighting up the area with floods. Swiftly it swooped down, came to ground a hundred yards away.

Harper, right arm in a sling, tumbled out and raced toward them.

"You didn't burn them!" he was yelling. "You didn't burn them!"

Mackenzie shook his head.

Harper pounded him on the back with his good hand. "Knew you wouldn't. Knew you wouldn't all the time. Just kidding the chief, eh? Having a little fun."

"Not exactly fun."

"About them trees," said Harper. "We can't take them back to Earth, after all."

"I told you that," Mackenzie said.

"Earth just called me, half an hour ago," said Harper. "Seems there's a law, passed centuries ago. Against bringing alien plants to Earth. Some lunkhead once brought a bunch of stuff from Mars that just about ruined Earth, so they passed the law. Been there all the time, forgotten."

Mackenzie nodded. "Someone dug it up."

"That's right," said Harper. "And slapped an injunction on Galactic. We can't touch those trees."

"You wouldn't have anyhow," said Mackenzie. "They wouldn't go."

"But you made the deal! They were anxious to go—"

"That," Mackenzie told him, "was before they found out we used plants for food—and other things."

"But... but—"

"To them," said Mackenzie, "we're just a gang of ogres. Something they'll scare the little plants with. Tell them if they don't be quiet the humans will get 'em."

Nellie came around the corner of the tractor, still hauling the Encyclopedia by his topknot.

"Hey," yelled Harper, "what goes on here?"

"We'll have to build a concentration camp," said Mackenzie. "Big high fence." He motioned with his thumb toward the Encyclopedia.

Harper stared. "But he hasn't done anything!"

"Nothing but try to take over the human race," Mackenzie said.

Harper sighed. "That makes two fences we got to build. That rifle tree back at the post is shooting up the place."

Mackenzie grinned. "Maybe the one fence will do for the both of them."

Atomic war can produce
strange situations—for an atomic bomb
can explode more than once! And it may be that the
victims of the attack dare not reply!

# Thunder and Roses

**By Theodore Sturgeon**

Illustrated by Elliot

When Pete Mawser learned about the show, he turned away from the GHQ bulletin board, touched his long chin, and determined to shave. This was odd, because the show would be video, and he would see it in his barracks.

He had an hour and a half. It felt good to have a purpose again—even shaving before eight o'clock. Eight o'clock Tuesday, just the way it used to be. Everyone used to catch that show on Tuesday. Everyone used to say, Wednesday morning: "How about the way she sang 'The Breeze and I' last night?" "Hey—did you hear Starr last night?"

That was a while ago, before all those people were dead, before the country was dead. Starr Anthim, institution, like Crosby, like Duse, like Jenny Lind, like the Statue of Liberty.

(Liberty had been one of the first to get it, her bronze beauty volatilized, radioactive, and even now being carried about in vagrant winds, spreading over the earth—)

Pete Mawser grunted and forced his thoughts away from the drifting, poisonous fragments of a blasted Liberty. Hate was first. Hate was ubiquitous, like the increasing blue glow in the air at night, like the tension that hung over the base.

Gunfire crackled sporadically far to the right, swept nearer. Pete stepped out of the street and made for a parked ten wheeler. There's a lot of cover in and around a ten wheeler.

There was a Wac sitting on the short running board.

At the corner a stocky figure backed into the intersection. The man carried a toddy-gun in his arms, and he was swinging it to and fro with the gentle, wavering motion of a weathervane. He staggered toward them, his gun muzzle hunting. Someone fired from a building and the man swiveled and blasted wildly at the sound.

"He's—blind," said Pete Mawser, and added, "He ought to be," looking at the tattered face.

A siren keened. An armored jeep slewed into the street. The full-throated roar of a brace of .50 caliber machine guns put a swift and shocking end to the incident.

"Poor crazy kid," Pete said softly. "That's the fourth I've seen today." He looked down at the Wac. She was smiling.

"Hey!"

"Hello, Sarge." She must have identified him before, because now she did not raise her eyes nor her voice. "What happened?"

"You know what happened. Some kid got tired of having nothing to fight and nowhere to run to. What's the matter with you?"

"No," she said. "I don't mean that." At last she looked up at him. "I mean all of this. I can't seem to remember."

"You . . . well, gee, it's not easy to forget. We got hit. We got hit everywhere at once. All the big cities are gone. We got it from both sides. We got too much. The air is becoming radioactive. We'll all—" He checked himself. She didn't know. She'd forgotten. There was nowhere to escape to, and she'd escaped inside herself, right here. Why tell her about it? Why tell her that everyone was going to die? Why tell her that other, shameful thing: that we hadn't struck back?

But she wasn't listening. She was still looking at him. Her eyes were not quite straight. One held his but the other was slightly shifted and seemed to be looking at his temple. She was smiling again. When his voice trailed off she didn't prompt him. Slowly, he moved away. She did not turn her head, but kept looking up at where he had been, smiling a little. He turned away, wanting to run, walking fast.

(How long can a guy hold out? When you're in the army they try to make you be like everybody else. What do you do when everybody else is cracking up?)

He blanked out the mental picture of himself as the last one left sane. He'd followed that one through before. It always led to the conclusion that it would be better to be one of the first. He wasn't ready for that yet.

Then he blanked that out, too. Every time he said to himself that he wasn't ready for that yet, something within him asked "why not?" and he never seemed to have an answer ready.

(How long could a guy hold out?)

He climbed the steps of the QM Central and went inside. There was nobody at the reception switchboard. It didn't matter. Messages were carried by guys in jeeps, or on motorcycles. The Base Command was not insisting that anybody stick to a sitting job these days. Ten deskmen would crack up for every one on a jeep, or on the soul-sweat squads. Pete made up his mind to put in a little stretch on a squad tomorrow. Do him good. He just hoped that this time the adjutant wouldn't burst into tears in the middle of the parade ground. You could keep your mind on the manual of arms just fine until something like that happened.

He bumped into Sonny Weisefreund in the barracks corridor. The tech's round young face was as cheerful as ever. He was naked and glowing, and had a towel thrown over his shoulder.

"Hi, Sonny. Is there plenty of hot water?"

"Why not?" grinned Sonny. Pete grinned back, cursing inwardly. Could anybody say anything about anything at all without one of the reminders? Sure there was hot water. The QM barracks had hot water for three hundred men. There were three dozen left. Men dead, men gone to the hills, men locked up so they wouldn't—

"Starr Anthim's doing a show tonight."

"Yeah. Tuesday night. Not funny, Pete. Don't you know there's a war—"

"No kidding," Pete said swiftly. "She's here—right here on the base."

Sonny's face was joyful. "Gee." He pulled the towel off his shoulder and tied it around his waist. "Starr Anthim here! Where are they going to put on the show?"

"HQ, I imagine. Video only. You know about public gatherings." And a good thing, too, he thought. Put on an in-person show, and some torn-up GI would crack during one of her numbers. He himself would get plenty mad over a thing like that—mad enough to do something about it then and there. And there would probably be a hundred and fifty or more like him, going raving mad because someone had spoiled a Starr Anthim show. That would be a dandy little shamble for her to put in her memory book.

"How'd she happen to come here, Pete?"

"Drifted in on the last gasp of a busted-up Navy helicopter."

"Yeah, but why?"

"Search me. Get your head out of that gift-horse's mouth."

He went into the washroom, smiling and glad that he still could. He undressed and put his neatly folded clothes down on a bench. There were a soap wrapper and an empty toothpaste tube lying near the wall. He went and picked them up and put them in the catchall. He took the mop which leaned against the partition and mopped the floor where Sonny had splashed after shaving. Got to keep things squared away. He might say something if it were anyone else but Sonny. But Sonny wasn't cracking up. Sonny always had been like that. Look there. Left his razor out again.

Pete started his shower, meticulously adjusting the valves until the pressure and temperature exactly suited him. He didn't do anything slapdash these days. There was so much to feel, and taste, and see now. The impact of water on his skin, the smell of soap, the consciousness of light and heat, the very pressure of standing on the soles of his feet—he wondered vaguely how the slow increase of radioactivity in the air, as the nitrogen transmuted to Carbon Fourteen, would affect him if he kept carefully healthy in every way. What happens first? Do you go blind? Headaches, maybe? Perhaps you lose your appetite. Or maybe you get tired all the time.

Why not go look it up?

On the other hand, why bother? Only a very small percentage of the men would die of radioactive poisoning. There were too many other things that killed more quickly, which was probably just as well. That razor, for example. It lay gleaming in a sunbeam, curved and clean in the yellow light.

Sonny's father and grandfather had used it, or so he said, and it was his pride and joy.

Pete turned his back on it, and soaped under his arms, concentrating on the tiny kisses of bursting bubbles. In the midst of a recurrence of disgust at himself for thinking so often of death, a staggering truth struck him. He did not think of such things because he was morbid, after all! It was the very familiarity of things that brought death-thoughts. It was either "I shall never do this again" or "This is one of the last times I shall do this." You might devote yourself completely to doing things in different ways, he thought madly. You might crawl across the floor this time, and next time walk across on your hands. You might skip dinner tonight, and have a snack at two in the morning instead, and eat grass for breakfast.

But you had to breathe. Your heart had to beat. You'd sweat and you'd shiver, the same as always. You couldn't get away from that. When those things happened, they would remind you. Your heart wouldn't beat out its *wunklunk, wunklunk* any more. It would go *one-less one-less*, until it yelled and yammered in your ears and you had to make it stop.

Terrific polish on that razor.

And your breath would go on, same as before. You could sidle through this door, back through the next one and the one after, and figure out a totally new way to go through the one after that, but your breath would keep on sliding in and out of your nostrils like a razor going through whiskers, making a sound like a razor being stropped.

Sonny came in. Pete soaped his hair. Sonny picked up

the razor and stood looking at it. Pete watched him, soap ran into his eye, he swore, and Sonny jumped.

"What are you looking at, Sonny? Didn't you ever see it before?"

"Oh, sure. Sure. I just was—" He shut the razor, opened it, flashed light from its blade, shut it again. "I'm tired of using this, Pete. I'm going to get rid of it. Want it?"

Want it? In his foot locker, maybe. Under his pillow. "Thanks no, Sonny. Couldn't use it."

"I like safety razors," Sonny mumbled. "Electrics, even better. What are we going to do with it?"

"Throw it in the . . . no." Pete pictured the razor turning end over end in the air, half open, gleaming in the maw of the catchall. "Throw it out the —" No. Curving out into the long grass. You might want it. You might crawl around in the moonlight looking for it. You might find it.

"I guess maybe I'll break it up."

"No."Pete said. "The pieces—" Sharp little pieces. Hollow-ground fragments. "I'll think of something. Wait'll I get dressed."

He washed briskly, toweled, while Sonny stood looking at the razor. It was a blade now, and if you broke it, there would be shards and glittering splinters, still razor sharp. You could slap its edge into an emery wheel and grind it away, and somebody could find it and put another edge on it because it was so obviously a razor, a fine steel razor, one that would slice so— "I know. The laboratory. We' ll get rid of it," Pete said confidently.

He stepped into his clothes, and together they went to the laboratory wing. It was very quiet there. Their voices echoed.

"One of the ovens," said Pete, reaching for the razor.

"Bake ovens? Your're crazy!"

Pete chuckled. "You don't know this place, do you? Like everything else on the base, there was a lot more went on here than most people knew about. They kept calling it the bake shop. Well, it *was* research headquarters for new high-nutrient flours. But there's lots else here. We tested utensils and designed beet peelers and all sorts of things like that. There's an electric furnace in here that—" He pushed open a door.

They crossed a long, quiet, clutter room to the thermal equipment. "We can do everything here from annealing glass, through glazing ceramics, to finding the melting point of frying pans." He clicked a switch tentatively. A pilot light glowed. He swung open a small, heavy door and set the razor inside. "Kiss it good-by. In twenty minutes it'll be a puddle."

"I want to see that," said Sonny. "Can I look around until its's cooked?"

"Why not?"

(Everybody around here always said: "Why not?")

They walked through the laboratories. Beautifully equipped, they were, and too quiet. Once they passed a major who was bent over a complex electronic hookup on one of the benches. He was watching a little amber light flicker, and he did not return their salute. They tiptoed past him, feeling awed at his absorption, envying it. They saw the models of the automatic kneaders, the vitaminizers, the remote signal thermostats and timers and controls.

"What's in there?"

"I dunno. I'm over the edge of my territory. I don't think there's anybody left for this section. They were mostly mechanical and electronic theoreticians. The only thing I know about them is that if we ever needed anything in the way of tools, meters, or equipment, they had it or something better, and if we ever got real bright and figured out a startling new idea, they'd already have built it and junked it a month ago. Hey!"

Sonny followed the pointing hand. "What?"

"That wall section. It's loose, or . . . well, what do you know?"

He pushed at the section of a wall, which was very slightly out of line. There was a dark space beyond.

"What's in there?"

"Nothing, or some semiprivate hush-hush job. These guys used to get away with murder."

Sonny said, with an uncharacteristic flash of irony, "Isn't that the Army theoretician's business?"

Cautiously they peered in, then entered.

"Wh . . . *hey!* The door!"

It swung swiftly and quietly shut. The soft click of the latch was accompanied by a blaze of light.

The room was small and windowless. It contained machinery—a "trickle" charger, a bank of storage batteries, an electric-powered dynamo, two small self-starting gas-driven light plants and a Diesel complete with sealed compressed-air starting cylinders. In the corner was a relay rack with its panel-bolts spot-welded. Protruding from it was a red-top lever. Nothing was labeled.

They looked at the equipment wordlessly for a time and then Sonny said, "Somebody wanted to make awful sure he had power for something."

"Now, I wonder what—" Pete walked over to the relay rack. He looked at the lever without touching it. It was wired up; behind the handle, on the wire, was a folded tag. He opened it cautiously. "To be used only on specific orders of the Commanding Officer."

"Give it a yank and see what happens."

Something clicked behind them. "What was that?"

"Seemed to come from that rig beside the door."

They approached it cautiously. There was a spring-loaded solenoid attached to a bar which was hinged to drop across the inside of the secret door, where it would fit into steel grudgeons on the panel.

It clicked again. "A Geiger," said Pete disgustedly.

"Now why," mused Sonny, "would they design a door to stay locked unless the general radioactivity went beyond a certain point? That's what it is. See the relays? And the overload switch there? And this?"

"It has a manual lock, too," Pete pointed out. The counter clicked again. "Let's get out of here. I got one of those things built into my head, these days."

The door opened easily. They went out, closing it behind them. The keyhole was cleverly concealed in the crack between two boards.

They were silent as they made their way back to the QM labs. The small thrill of violation was gone, and, for Pete Mawser at least, the hate was back, that and the shame. A few short weeks before, this base had been a part of the finest country on earth. There was a lot of work here that was secret, and a lot that was such purely progressive and unapplied research that it would be in the way anywhere else but in this quiet wilderness.

Sweat stood out on his forehead. They hadn't struck back at their murderers! It was quite well known that there were launching sites all over the country, in secret caches far from any base or murdered city. Why must they sit here waiting to die, only to let the enemy—"enemies" was more like it—take over the continent when it was safe again?

He smiled grimly. One small consolation. They'd hit too hard; that was a certainty. Probably each of the attackers underestimated what the other would throw. The results—a spreading transmutation of nitrogen into deadly Carbon Fourteen. The effects would not be limited to the continent. What ghastly long-range effect the muted radioactivity would have on the overseas enemies was something that no one alive today could know.

Back at the furnace, Pete glanced at the temperature dial, then kicked the latch control. The pilot winked out, and then the door swung open. They blinked and started back from the raging heat within, then bent and peered. The razor was gone. A pool of brilliance lay on the floor of the compartment.

"Ain't much left. Most of it oxidized away," Pete grunted.

They stood together for a time with their faces lit by that small shimmering ruin. Later, as they walked back to the barracks, Sonny broke his long silence with a sigh. "I'm glad we did that, Pete. I'm awful glad we did that."

At a quarter to eight they were waiting before the combination console in the barracks. All hands except Pete and Sonny and a wiry-haired, thick-set corporal named Bonze had elected to see the show on the big screen in the mess hall. The reception was better there, of course, but, as Bonze put it, "you don't get close enough in a big place like that."

"I hope she's the same," said Sonny, half to himself.

Why should she be? thought Pete morosely as he turned on the set and watched the screen begin to glow. There were many more of the golden speckles that had killed reception for the past two weeks. Why should anything be the same, ever again?

He fought a sudden temptation to kick the set to pieces. It, and Starr Anthim, were part of something that was dead. The country was dead, a real country—prosperous, sprawling, laughing, grabbing, growing and changing, leprous in spots with poverty and injustice, but healthy enough to overcome any ill. He wondered how the murders would like it. They were welcome to it, now. Nowhere to go. No one to fight. That was true for every soul on earth now.

"You hope she's the same," he muttered.

"The show, I mean," said Sonny mildly. "I'd like to just sit here and have it like... like—"

Oh, thought Pete mistily. Oh—that. Somewhere to go,

that's what it is, for a few minutes. "I know," he said, all the harshness gone from his voice.

Noise receded from the audio as the carrier swept in. The light on the screen swirled and steadied into a diamond pattern. Pete adjusted the focus, chromic balance and intensity. "Turn out the lights, Bonze. I don't want to see anything but Starr Anthim."

It *was* the same, at first. Starr Anthim had never used the usual fanfares, fade-ins, color and clamor of her contemporaries. A black screen, then *click!* a blaze of gold. It was all there, in focus; tremendously intense, it did not change. Rather, the eye changed to take it in. She never moved for seconds after she came on; she was there, a portrait, a still face and a white throat. Her eyes were open and sleeping. Her face was alive and still.

Then, in the eyes which seemed green but were blue flecked with gold, an awareness seemed to gather, and they came awake. Only then was it noticeable that her lips were parted. Something in the eyes made the lips be seen, though nothing moved yet. Not until she bent her head slowly, so that some of the gold flecks seemed captured in the golden brows. The eyes were not, then, looking out at an audience. They were looking at me, and at *me*, and at ME.

"Hello—you," she said. She was a dream, with a kid sister's slightly irregular teeth.

Bonze shuddered. The cot on which he lay began to squeak rapidly. Sonny shifted in annoyance. Pete reached out in the dark and caught the leg of the cot. The squeaking subsided.

"May I sing a song?" Starr asked. There was music, very faint. "It's an old one, and one of the best. It's an easy song, a deep song, one that comes from the part of men and women that is mankind—the part that has in it no greed, no hate, no fear. This song is about joyousness and strength. It's—my favorite. Isn't it yours?"

The music swelled. Pete recognized the first two notes of the introduction and swore quietly. This was wrong. This song was not for. . . this song was part of—

Sonny sat raptly. Bonze lay still.

Starr Anthim began to sing. Her voice was deep and powerful, but soft, with the merest touch of vibrato at the ends of the phrases. The song flowed from her, without noticeable effort, seeming to come from her face, her long hair, her wide-set eyes. Her voice, like her face, was shadowed and clean, round, blue and green but mostly gold:

*"When you gave me your heart,*
*you gave me the world,*
*you gave me the night and the day,*
*and thunder, and roses, and sweet green grass,*
*the sea, and soft wet clay.*

*I drank the dawn from a golden*
*cup,*
*from a silver one, the dark,*
*the steed I rode was the wild west*
*wind,*
*my song was the brook and the*
*lark."*

The music spiraled, caroled, slid into a somber cry of muted, hungry sixths and ninths; rose, blared, and cut, leaving her voice full and alone:

*"With thunder I smote the evil of earth, with roses I won the right, with the sea I washed, and with clay I built, and the world was a place of light!"*

The last note left a face perfectly composed again, and there was no movement in it; it was sleeping and vital while the music curved off and away to the places where music rests when it is not heard.

Starr smiled.

"It's so easy," she said. "So simple. All that is fresh and clean and strong about mankind is in that song, and I think that's all that need concern us about mankind." She leaned forward. "Don't you see?"

The smile faded and was replaced with a gentle wonder. A tiny furrow appeared between her brows; she drew back quickly. "I can't seem to talk to you tonight," she said, her voice small. "You hate something."

Hate was shaped like a monstrous mushroom. Hate was the random speckling of a video plate.

"What has happened to us," said Starr abruptly, impersonally "is simple, too. It doesn't matter who did it—do you understand that? *It doesn't matter*. We were attacked. We were struck from the east and from the west. Most of the bombs were atomic—there were blast bombs and there were dust bombs. We were hit by about five hundred and thirty bombs altogether, and it has killed us."

She waited.

Sonny's fist smacked into his palm. Bonze lay with his eyes open, quiet. Pete's jaws hurt.

"We have more bombs than both of them put together. We *have* them. We are not going to use them. *Wait!*" She raised her hands suddenly, as if she could see into each man's face. They sank back, tense.

"So saturated is the atmosphere with Carbon Fourteen that all of us in this hemisphere are going to die. Don't be afraid to say it. Don't be afraid to think it. It is the truth, and it must be faced. As the transmutation effect spreads from the ruins of our cities, the air will become increasingly radioactive, and then we must die. In months, in a year or so, the effects will be strong overseas. Most of the people there will die, too. None will escape completely. A worse thing will come to them than anything they gave us, because there will be a wave of horror and madness which is impossible to us. They will live and burn and sicken, and the children that will be born to them—" She shook her head, and her lower lip grew full. She visibly pulled herself together.

"Five hundred and thirty bombs— I don't think either of our attackers knew just how strong the other was. There has been so much secrecy." Her voice was sad. She shrugged slightly. "They have killed us, and they have ruined themselves. As for us—we are not blameless, either. Neither are we helpless to do anything—yet. But what we must do is hard. We must die—without striking back."

She gazed briefly at each man in turn, from the screen. "We must *not* strike back. Mankind is about to go through a hell of his own making. We can be vengeful—or merciful, if you like—and let go with the hundreds of bombs we have. That would sterilize the planet so that not a microbe, not a blade of grass could escape, and nothing new could grow. We would reduce the earth to a bald thing, dead and deadly.

"No—it just won't do. We can't do it.

"Remember the song? *That* is humanity. That's in all humans. A disease made other humans our enemies for a time, but as the generations march past, enemies become friends and friends enemies. The enmity of those who have killed us is such a tiny, temporary thing in the long sweep of history!"

Her voice deepened. "Let us die with the knowledge that we have done the one noble thing left to us. The spark of humanity can still live and grow on this planet. It will be blown and drenched, shaken and all but extinguished, but it will live if that song is a true one. It will live if we are human enough to discount the fact that the spark is in the custody of our temporary enemy. Some—a few—of his children will live to merge with the new humanity that will gradually emerge from the jungles and the wilderness. Perhaps there will be ten thousand years of beastliness; perhaps man will be able to rebuild while he still has his ruins."

She raised her head, her voice tolling. "And even if this is the end of humankind, we dare not take away the chances some other life form might have to succeed where we failed. If we retaliate, there will not be a dog, a deer, an ape, a bird or fish or lizard to carry the evolutionary torch. In the name of justice, if we must condemn and destroy ourselves, let us not condemn all life along with us! We are heavy enough with sins. If we must destroy, let us stop with destroying ourselves!"

There was a shimmering flicker of music. It seemed to stir her hair like a breath of wind. She smiled.

"That's all," she whispered. And to each man there she said, "Good night—"

The screen went black. As the carrier cut off—there was no announcement—the ubiquitous speckles began to swarm across it.

Pete rose and switched on the lights. Bonze and Sonny, were quite still. It must have been minutes later when Sonny sat up straight, shaking himself like a puppy. Something besides the silence seemed to tear with the movement.

He said, softly: "You're not allowed to fight anything, or to run away, or to live, and now you can't even hate any more, because Staff says 'no.'"

There was bitterness in the sound of it, and a bitter smell to the air.

Pete Mawser sniffed once, which had nothing to do with the smell. He froze, sniffed again. "What's that smell, Son?"

Sonny tested it. "I don't — Something familiar. Vanilla — no . . . No."

"Almonds. Bitter— *Bonze!*"

Bonze lay still with his eyes open grinning. His jaw muscles were knotted, and they could see almost all his teeth. He was soaking wet.

"Bonze!"

"It was just when she came on and said 'Hello—you, remember?" whispered Pete. "Oh, the poor kid. That's why he wanted to catch the show here instead of in the mess hall."

"Went out looking at her," said Sonny through pale lips. "I. . . can't say I blame him much. Wonder where he got the stuff."

"Never mind that!" Pete's voice was harsh. "Let's get out of here."

They left to call the meat wagon. Bonze lay watching the console with his dead eyes and his smell of bitter almonds.

Pete did not realize where he was going, or exactly why, until he found himself on the dark street near GHQ and the communications shack. It had something to do with Bonze. Not that he wanted to do what Bonze had done. But then, he hadn't thought of it. What would he have done if he'd thought of it? Nothing, probably. But still—it might be nice to be able to hear Starr, and see her, whenever he felt like it. Maybe there weren't any recordings; yet her musical background was recorded, and the Sig might have dubbed the show off.

He stood uncertainly outside the GHQ building. There was a cluster of men outside the main entrance. Pete smilled briefly. Rain, nor snow, nor sleet, nor gloom of night could stay the stage-door Johnnie.

He went down the side street and up the delivery ramp in the back. Two doors along the platform was the rear exit of the communications section.

There was a light on in the communications shack. He had his hand out to the screen door when he noticed someone standing in the shadows beside it. The light played daintily on the golden margins of a head and face.

He stopped. "Starr Anthim!"

"Hello, soldier. Sergeant."

He blushed like an adolescent. "I—" His voice left him. He swallowed, reached up to whip off his hat. He had no hat. "I saw the show," he said. He felt clumsy. It was dark, and yet he was very conscious of the fact that his dress shoes were indifferently shined.

She moved toward him into the light, and she was so beautiful that he had to close his eyes. "What's your name?"

"Mawser. Pete Mawser."

"Like the show?"

Not looking at her, he said stubbornly, "No."

"Oh?"

"I mean . . . I liked it some. The song."

"I . . . think I see."

"I wondered if I could maybe get a recording."

"I think so," she said. "What kind of a reproducer have you got?"

"Audiovid."

"A disk. Yes; we dubbed off a few. Wait, I'll get you one."

She went inside, moving slowly. Pete watched her, spellbound. She was a silhouette, crowned and haloed; and then she was a framed picture, vivid and golden. He waited, watching the light hungrily. She returned with a large envelope, called good night to someone inside, and came out on the platform.

"Here you are, Pete Mawser."

"Thanks very—" he mumbled. He wet his lips. "It was very good of you."

"Not really. The more it circulates, the better." She laughed suddenly. "That isn't meant quite as it sounds. I'm not exactly looking for new publicity these days."

The stubborness came back. "I don't know that you'd get it, if you put on that show in normal times."

Her eyebrows went up. "Well!" she smiled. "I seem to have made quite an impression."

"I'm sorry," he said warmly. "I shouldn't have taken that tack. Everything you think and say these days is exaggerated."

"I know what you mean." She looked around. "How is it here?"

"It's O.K. I used to be bothered by the secrecy, and being buried miles away from civilization." He chuckled bitterly. "Turned out to be lucky after all."

"You sound like the first chapter of 'One World or None'"

He looked up quickly. "What do you use for a reading list—the Government's own *'Index Expurgatorius'?*"

She laughed. "Come now—it isn't as bad as all that. The book was never banned. It was just—"

"—unfashionable," he filed in.

"Yes, more's the pity. If people had paid more attention to it in the Forties, perhaps this wouldn't have happened."

He followed her gaze to the dimly pulsating sky. "How long are you going to be here?"

"Until . . . as long as . . . I'm not leaving."

"You're not?"

"I'm finished," she said simply. "I've covered all the ground I can. I've been everywhere that . . . anyone knows about."

"With this show?"

She nodded. "With this particular message."

He was quiet, thinking. She turned to the door, and he put out his hand, not touching her. "Please— "

"What is it?"

"I'd like to . . . I mean, if you don't mind, I don't often have a chance to talk to — Maybe you'd like to walk around a little before you turn in."

"Thanks, no sergeant. I'm tired." She did sound tired. "I'll see you around."

He stared at her, a sudden fierce light in his brain. "I know where it is. It's got a red-topped lever and a tag referring to orders of the commanding officer. It's really camouflaged."

She was quiet so long that he thought she had not heard him. Then, "I'll take that walk."

They went down the ramp together and turned toward the dark parade ground.

"How did you know?" she asked quietly.

"Not too tough. This 'message' of yours; the fact that you've been all over the country with it; most of all, the fact that somebody finds it necessary to persuade us not to strike back. Who are you working for?" he asked bluntly.

Surprisingly, she laughed.

"What's that for?"

"A moment ago you were blusing and shuffling your feet."

His voice was rough. "I wasn't talking to a human being. I was talking to a thousand songs I've heard, and a hundred thousand blond pictures I've seen pinned up. You'd better tell me what this is all about."

She stopped. "Let's go up and see the colonel."

He took her elbow. "No. I'm just a sergeant, and he's high brass, and that doesn't make any difference at all now. You're a human being, and so am I, and I'm supposed to respect your rights as such. I don't. You're a woman, and— "

She stiffened. He kept her walking, and finished, "—and that will make as much difference as I let it. You'd better tell me about it."

"All right," she said, with a tired acquiescence that frightened something inside him. "You seem to have guessed right, though. It's true. There are master firing keys for the launching sites. We have located and dismantled all but two. It's very likely that one of the two was vaporized. The other one is—lost."

"Lost?"

"I don't have to tell you about the secrecy," she said disgustedly. "You know how it developed between nation and nation. You must know that it existed between State and Union, between department and department, office and office. There were only three or four men who knew where all the keys were. Three of them were in the Pentagon when it went up. That was the third blast bomb, you know. If there was another, it could only have been Senator Vandercook, and he died three weeks ago without talking."

"An automatic radio key, hm-m-m?"

"That's right. Sergeant, must we walk? I'm so tired— "

"I'm sorry," he said impulsively. They crossed to the reviewing stand and sat on the lonely benches. "Launching racks all over, all hidden, and all armed?"

"Most of them are armed. Enough. Armed and aimed."

"Aimed where?"

"It doesn't matter."

"I think I see. What's the optimum number again?"

"About six hundred and forty; a few more or less. At least five hundred and thirty have been thrown so far. We don't know exactly."

"Who are *we?*" he asked furiously.

"Who? Who?" She laughed weakly. "I could say, 'The Government,' perhaps. If the president dies, the vice president takes over, and then the secretary of state, and so on and on. How far can you go? Pete Mawser, don't you realize yet what's happened?"

"I don't know what you mean."

"How many people do you think are left in this country?"

"I don't know. Just a few million, I guess."

"How many are here?"

"About nine hundred."

"Then as far as I know, this is the largest city left."

He leaped to his feet. *"NO!"* The syllable roared away from him, hurled itself against the dark, empty buildings, came back to him in a series of lower-case echoes: no,no,no—*no*. . . *no*-no— n. . .

Starr began to speak rapidly, quietly. "They're scattered all over the fields and roads. They sit in the sun and die in the afternoon. They run in packs, they tear at each other. They pray and starve and kill themselves and die in the fires. The fires—everywhere, if anything stands, it's burning. Summer, and the leaves all down in the Berkshires, and the blue grass burnt brown; you can see the grass dying from the air, the death going out wider and wider from the bald spots. Thunder and roses... I saw roses, new ones, creeping from the smashed pots of a greenhouse. Brown petals, alive and sick, and the thorns turned back on themselves, growing into the stems, killing. Feldman died tonight."

He let her be quiet for a time. "Who is Feldman?"

"My pilot." She was talking hollowly into her hands. "He's been dying for weeks. He's been on his nerve-ends. I don't think he had any blood left. He buzzed your GHQ and made for the landing strip. He came in with the motor dead, free rotors, giro. Smashed the landing gear. He was dead, too. He killed a man in Chicago so he could steal gas. The man didn't want the gas. There was a dead girl by the pump. He didn't want us to go near. I'm not going anywhere. I'm going to stay here. I'm tired."

At last she cried.

Pete left her alone, and walked out to the center of the parade ground, looking back at the faint huddled glimmer on the bleachers. His mind flickered over the show that evening, and the way she had sung before the merciless transmitter. "Hello, you." "If we must destroy, let us stop with destroying ourselves!"

The dimming spark of humankind—what could it mean to her? How could it mean so much?

*"Thunder and roses."* Twisted sick, nonsurvival roses, killing themselves with their own thorns.

*"And the world was a place of light!"* Blue light, flickering in the contaminated air.

The enemy. The red-topped lever. Bronze. "They pray and starve and kill themselves and die in the fires."

What creatures were these, these corrupted, violent, murdering humans? What right had they to another chance? What was in them that was good?

Starr was good. Starr was crying. Only a human being could cry like that. Starr was a human being.

Had humanity anything of Starr Anthim in it?

Starr *was* a human being.

He looked down through the darkness for his hands. No planet, no universe, is greater to a man than his own ego, his own observing self. These hands were the hands of all history, and like the hands of all men, they could by their small acts make human history or end it. Whether this power of hands was that of a billion hands, or whether it came to a focus in these two—this was suddenly unimportant to the eternities which now infolded him.

He put humanity's hands deep in his pockets and walked slowly back to the bleachers.

"Starr."

She responded with a sleepy child, interrogative whimper.

"They'll get their chance, Starr. I won't touch the key."

She sat straight. She rose, and came to him, smiling. He could see her smile, because, very faintly in this air, her teeth flouoresced. She put her hands on his shoulders. "Pete."

He held her very close for a moment. Her knees buckled then, and he had to carry her.

There was no one in the Officers' Club, which was the nearest bulding. He stumbled in, moved clawing along the wall until he found a switch. The light hurt him. He carried her to a settee and put her down gently. She did not move. One side of her face was as pale as milk.

There was blood on his hands.

He stood looking stupidly at it, wiped it on the wides of his trousers, looking dully at Starr. There was blood on her shirt.

The echo of No's came back to him from the far walls of the big room before he knew he had spoken. Starr wouldn't do this. She couldn't!

A doctor. But there was no doctor. Not since Anders had hung himself. Get somebody. *Do* something.

He dropped to his knees and gently unbuttoned her shirt. Between the sturdy, unfeminine GI bra and the top of her slacks, there was blood on her side. He slipped out a clean handerchief and began to wipe it away. There was no wound, no puncture. But abruptly there was blood again. He blotted it carefully. And again there was blood.

It was like trying to dry a piece of ice with a towel.

He ran to the water cooler, wrung out the bloody handkerchief and ran back to her. He bathed her face carefully, the pale right side, the flushed left side. The handkerchief reddened again, this time with cosmetics, and then her face was pale all over, with great blue shadows under the eyes. While he watched, blood appeared on her left cheek.

There must be *somebody* — He fled to the door.

"Pete!"

Running, turning at the sound of her voice, he hit the doorpost stunningly, caromed off, flailed for his balance, and then was back at her side. "Starr! Hang on, now! I'll get a doctor as quick as—"

Her hand strayed over her left cheek. "You found out. Nobody else knew, but Feldman. It got hard to cover properly." Her hand went up to her hair.

"Starr, I'll get a—"

"Pete, darling, promise me something?"

"Why, sure; certainly, Starr."

"Don't disturb my hair. It isn't—all mine, you see." She sounded like a seven-year-old, playing a game. "It all came out on this side, you see? I don't want you to see me that way."

He was on his knees beside her again. "What is it? What happened to you?" he asked hoarsely.

"Philadelphia," she murmured. "Right at the beginning. The mushroom went up a half-mile away. The studio caved in. I came to the next day. I didn't know I was burned, then. It didn't show. My left side. It doesn't matter, Pete. It doesn't hurt at all, now."

He sprang to his feet again. "I'm going for a doctor."

"Don't go away. Please don't go away and leave me. Please don't." There were tears in her eyes. "Wait just a little while. Not very long, Pete."

He sank to his knees again. She gathered both his hands in hers and held them tightly. She smilled happily. "You're good, Pete. You're so good."

(She couldn't hear the blood in his ears, the roar of the whirlpool of hate and fear and anguish that spun inside him.)

She talked to him in a low voice, and then in whispers. Sometimes he hated himself because he couldn't quite follow her. She talked about school, and her first audition. "I was so scared that I got a vibrato in my voice. I'd never had one before. I always let myself get a little scared when I sing now. It's easy." There was something about a windowbox when

she was four years old. "Two real live tulips and a pitcher-plant. I used to be sorry for the flies."

There was a long period of silence after that during which his muscles throbbed with cramp and stiffness, and gradually became numb. He must have dozed; he awoke with a violent start, feeling her fingers on his face. She was propped up on one elbow. She said clearly, "I just wanted to tell you, darling. Let me go first, and get everything ready for you. It's going to be wonderful. I'll fix you a special tossed salad. I'll make you a steamed chocolate pudding and keep it hot for you."

Too muddled to understand what she was saying, he smiled and pressed her back on the settee. She took his hands again.

The next time he awoke it was broad daylight, and she was dead.

Sonny Weisefreund was sitting on his cot when he got back to the barracks. He handed over the recording he had picked up from the parade ground on the way back. "Dew on it. Dry it off. Good boy," he croaked, and fell face downward on the cot Bonze had used.

Sonny stared at him. "Pete! Where've you been? What happened? Are you all right?"

Pete shifted a little and grunted. Sonny shrugged and took the audiovid disk out of its wet envelope. Moisture would not harm it particularly, though it could not be played while wet. It was made of a fine spiral of plastic, insulated between laminations. Electrostatic pickups above and below the turntable would fluctuate with changes in the dielectric constant which had been impressed by the recording, and these changes were amplified for the scanners. The audio was a conventional hill-and-dale needle. Sonny began to wipe it down carefully.

Pete fought upward out of a vast, green-lit place full of flickering cold fires. Starr was calling him. Something was punching him, too. He fought it weakly, trying to hear what she was saying. But someone else was jabbering too loud for him to hear.

He opened his eyes. Sonny was shaking him, his round face pink with excitement. The audiovid was running. Starr was talking. Sonny got up impatiently and turned down the audio gain. "Pete! Pete! Wake up, will you? I got to tell you something. Listen to me! Wake up, will yuh?"

"Huh?"

"That's better. Now listen. I've just been listening to Starr Anthim— "

"She's dead," said Pete. Sonny didn't hear. He went on, explosively, "I've figured it out. Starr was sent out here, and all over, to *beg* someone not to fire any more atom bombs. If the government was sure they wouldn't strike back, they wouldn't have taken the trouble. Somewhere, Pete, there's some way to launch bombs at those murdering cowards—and I've got a pret-ty shrewd idea of how to do it."

Pete strained groggily toward the faint sound of Starr's voice. Sonny talked on. "Now, s'posing there was a master radio key—an automatic code device something like the alarm signal they have on ships, that rings a bell on any ship within radio range when the operator sends four long dashes. Suppose there's an automatic code machine to launch bombs, with repeaters, maybe, buried all over the country. What would it be? Just a little lever to pull; thass all. How would the thing be hidden? In the middle of a lot of other equipment, that's where; in some place where you'd expect to find crazy-looking secret stuff. Like an experiment station. Like right here. You beginning to get the idea?"

"Shut up. I can't hear her."

"The hell with her! You can hear her some other time. You didn't hear a thing I said!"

"She's dead."

"Yeah. Well, I figure I'll pull that handle. What can I lose? It'll give those murderin'. . . *what?*"

"She's dead."

"Dead? Starr Anthim?" His young face twisted, Sonny sank down to the cot. "You're half asleep. You don't know what you're saying."

"She's dead," Pete said hoarsely. "She got burned by one of the first bombs. I was with her when she . . . she— Shut up, now, and get out of here and let me listen!" he bellowed hoarsely.

Sonny stood up slowly. "They killed her, too. They killed her. That does it. That just fixes it up." His face was white. He went out.

Pete got up. His legs weren't working right. He almost fell. He brought up against the console with a crash, his outflung arm sending the pickup skittering across the record. He put it on again and turned up the gain, then lay down to listen.

His head was all mixed up. Sonny talked too much. Bomb launchers, automatic code machines—

*"You gave me your heart,"* sang Starr. *"You gave me your heart. You gave me your heart. You–"*

Pete heaved himself up again and moved the pickup arm. Anger, not at himself, but at Sonny for causing him to cut the disk that way, welled up.

Starr was talking, stupidly, her face going through the same expression over and over again. *"Struck from the east and from the Struck from the east and from the–"*

He got up again wearily and moved the pickup.

*You gave me your heart,"* sang Starr. *You gave me*

Pete made an agonized sound that was not a word at all, bent, lifted, and sent the console crashing over. In the bludgeoning silence he said, "I did, too."

Then, "Sonny." He waited.

*"Sonny!"*

His eyes went wide then, and he cursed and bolted for the corridor.

The panel was closed when he reached it. He kicked at it. It flew open, discovering darkness.

"Hey!" bellowed Sonny. "Shut it! You turned off the lights!"

Pete! What's the matter?"

"Nothing's the matter, Son," croaked Pete.

"What are you looking at?" said Sonny uneasily.

"I'm sorry," said Pete as gently as he could. "I just wanted to find something out, is all. Did you tell anyone else about this?" He pointed to the lever.

"Why no. I only just figured it out while you were sleeping, just now."

Pete looked around carefully while Sonny shifted his weight. Pete moved toward a tool rack. "Something you haven't noticed yet, Sonny," he said softly, and pointed. "Up there, on the wall behind you. High up. See?"

Sonny turned. In one fluid movement Pete plucked off a fourteen-inch box wrench and hit Sonny with it as hard as he could.

Afterward he went to work systematically on the power supplies. He pulled the plugs on the gas engines and cracked their cylinders with a maul. He knocked off the tubing of the Diesel starters—the tanks let go explosively—and he cut all the cables with bolt cutters. Then he broke up the relay rack and its lever. When he was quite finished, he put away his tools and bent and stroked Sonny's tousled hair.

He went out and closed the partition carefully. It certainly was a wonderful piece of camouflage. He sat down heavily on a workbench nearby.

"You'll have your chance," he said into the far future. "And by Heaven, you'd better make good."

After that he just waited.